THE CITY OF
SILVER LIGHT

Ruth Fox

THE CITY OF SILVER LIGHT

© 2012 and 2020 by Hague Publishing
First Edition (ebook) 2012
Second Edition (paperback) 2020

Hague Publishing
PO Box 451
Bassendean Western Australia 6934
Email: contact@haguepublishing.com
Web: www.haguepublishing.com

ISBN: 978-0-6485714-7-6

Cover Art: The City of Silver Light by Ruth Fox

Typeset Century Schoolbook 12/14

THE CITY OF SILVER LIGHT

" ... beautifully written with intriguing
world building ..."
Christina – Ensconced in Lit

"I love ... its delicious mix of genres;
allegory, family story, fantasy, science
fiction. ..."
Readalot

"I heartily recommend this book at any
reader who enjoys something a bit out of
the general line."
*Sally Odgers
(Children's and Teen Fiction Author)*

Dedication

This book is for my parents, Mark and Olga, who opened my mind to the wonders of art and literature; for my brother, Oliver, with whom I spent my childhood imagining other worlds; and for my amazing partner, Conan, whose belief in me keeps me going every moment.

Chapter 1
In the Park

ON a clear night of frost and ice she falls from the sky.

I see the brilliant flash of her descent from my bedroom window. I've been spying on Dad, who has been sitting in the car for three hours, chain-smoking. From here I can see the entire street block, and the dark shapes of the trees in the park across the road. I can also see straight through the frost-rimmed windscreen, where Dad's sadness glows in the streetlight.

Daniel's small huffing exhalations are setting the rhythm of the night, but I can't sleep when it's like this. Too silent: a tense silence, like somebody died. I'm thinking that the ice-covered world outside might actually be warmer than inside our house, even though they're calling this the coldest winter on record.

'It's global warming, Jake,' Sharna Devon enlightened me the other morning.

The primary school Daniel goes to is down the road from Cassidy Heights Secondary College, so we catch the same bus to school on most days. My friend Keira used to save us seats but when she started going out with Andrew Dempsey she dropped that habit pretty quickly. Just like she stopped coming round to our house to muck around after school, even though she'd been doing that since we were six.

Andrew is the jealous type – and not without cause. I've been in love with Keira for years.

I usually try to avoid Sharna Devon, but that day the bus was full and all the other seats were taken. I tried to tune her out, drawing snowflakes on the fogged-up bus window. 'All the climates are messed up, and the currents in the ocean are changing.' she droned. 'It's the end of the world. We'll have more earthquakes and volcano eruptions. Everyone who lives on the coast is going to get swamped when the ice caps melt.'

'Really?' I said, putting a finger to my chin and pursing my lips. 'But that would be good for the fish, right?'

She gave me a disappointed look. 'How old are you, Jake Miles?'

Later, I'd tried explaining the ozone layer and gas emissions to Daniel. My younger brother is still grappling with the idea that the world doesn't change just because you want it to. He furrowed his brow in consternation. 'Why don't we just make it stop, then? If it's such a bad thing, why don't we fix it?'

'If we're ever going to stop the effects, we'd have to stop driving cars. We'd have to stop making things in factories – that means books and Play Stations and DVDs – and we'd have to stop cutting down trees to make space for houses. Because everything we're doing just by living our everyday lives makes all this bad stuff. It'd be changing the way we live. It'd be like a different world.'

He'd pursed his lips, still confused. 'What about Dad's smoking?' he said at last. 'Is that making the hole in the ozone layer bigger?'

I told him yeah, and thought it was pretty funny when Nina yelled at him for burying Dad's Winfield Golds in the garden in the interests of environmental conservation.

But I'm wondering now if Sharna is right and this is the beginning of the end of the world – meteor showers, comets, space-junk falling in Phoenix Park. This flash – it traces a fiery path down below the canopies of the trees. I blink the bright blue afterimage from my eyes, and though Daniel's breathing continues uninterrupted, I know I haven't imagined it.

I throw the blanket off my shoulders and pull on my jacket over my t-shirt. Outside it is so cold that it drenches me like water. My breath clouds the air. The world has frozen in the chill of the night, and it is beautiful. Ice clings to the shrubs by the door, and the grass glitters with jewels under the streetlights.

I pull on my runners by the door, shivering and tucking my hands in my pockets, and sprint across the lawn, which crunches under my feet. The cars parked on the road all wear shrouds of white. The shadows of the pink flamingos in number forty-seven's front yard stretch sharply across the road. It's silent. The world is mine alone.

I cross the road in seven steps. If anything, it seems darker under the trees of the park. The silver moonlight dapples the frozen grass. I make my way past the playground, geometric shapes against the sky, eerily still. There is a bike path winding its way through flower beds towards the lake, and I jog along this until I can see the water. Large chunks of ice float on the still surface, reflecting the moonlight. And something else – a faint orange glow. The flickering of a dying ember. I suck in a breath, amazed. It is real.

I wade through the stiff reeds towards the spot. The light of the moon gives me a crisp, clear view.

A figure lies there, curled against the spiky reeds, eyes closed, her hair tumbling over her face, wearing a white dress and covered in frost. She's dead. She must be. Her skin is so pale, whiter than it should be even in the bleached moonlight.

The embers scattered around her hiss and crackle.

I kneel beside her and touch her shoulder. 'Wake up,' I say softly. School lectures about drug overdoses nag at the back of my mind.

But as I touch her, she seems to warm. Under my fingers, the frost on her dress is melting. The ice in her hair beads to water and runs in rivulets across her face, and her skin blushes with a dull pink. I stare at the transformation in wonder.

A strange feeling washes through me. I can almost feel a sudden lurching in my stomach, as if I've missed a step and I'm falling, but it's cut short as her eyelids flutter and snap open. With a sudden jerk, she rears upwards and away from me, but stumbles and crashes back to the ground.

'No!' I call. 'Hey! Stop –'

She cries out as I grab at her shoulder again, and I draw back. She stares at me, wide-eyed, terrified.

The cuffs and knees of my tracksuit pants are wet through now, and moisture is seeping in through the rips in my runners. I haven't even noticed until now how cold I am, but I unbutton my jacket, forcing myself to move slowly, not to startle her. My fingers refuse to move independently, numbed by the cold, but I shrug it off and hold it out to her.

She doesn't move, just stares at me. Those eyes! They are as blue as midnight, with the shimmering depth of water. I've never seen anything so unnervingly beautiful.

'Here,' I say, my voice constricted. 'Put this on.'

She continues to stare.

'I'm not going to hurt you,' I assure her. 'I'm a friend.'

I can't tell if she even understands me. A full minute passes before she moves, and it isn't to take the jacket. She leaps up and runs. I can't move fast enough to stop her. By the time I've gotten to my feet she has vanished. The night is empty.

At my feet, the last of the embers flicker and die.

Chapter 2
Dreams

ANGEL girl. That's what I call her in my mind. Our family isn't religious, but back when I was a little kid and I couldn't sleep, Mum would tell me stories about angels. About how we each had a guardian angel, and even if we couldn't see them, they were always there watching over us. It made me feel safe.

Later, when Daniel was born, she'd tell him the same stories and I would listen and pretend I wasn't.

'Sometimes,' he'd murmured once, sleepily, 'Sometimes when the light is right it looks like I've got two shadows. One of them must be my guardian angel.'

Later, when she started to get sick, Daniel, only six years old, tearfully asked why Mum's guardian angel wasn't looking after her.

'She is!' Mum had said. 'She's here by my side, every second of the day.'

She said this so Daniel wouldn't worry. Me, I had a hard time imagining how much use Mum's angel was, seeing as how she died three weeks after that, Leaving nothing but memories and empty spaces and boxes of clothes stacked in the garage.

But if there really are such things as angels, I think they would look just like this girl.

When I climb back into bed, shivering, after having shoved my soaking tracksuit pants into the laundry basket, everything seems normal. How can it be real? Girls do not actually fall from the sky in a ball of flame. It's just a vivid dream, I tell myself.

Dad is unshaven at the breakfast table, reading the newspaper over a cup of coffee, his tie askew. Nina is bustling, a sure sign that she's in a bad mood.

'The water heater is on the blink again so I can't even wash the dishes properly. I'll have to go out and fiddle with the temperature again. Did you put your clothes out for the Salvos?'

I nod. We've all gotten used to Nina wanting to give things away to charity. 'Throwing things in the bin is such a waste,' she always says. You can't walk with her past a council bin without having her click her tongue and mutter something about the evils of throwing away food. 'They're in the plastic bags in the laundry. Daniel's, too.'

'I was thinking I could clean out the garage today, Alex. There's probably plenty of stuff in there the charities could use.'

Dad abruptly puts his coffee down, folds his newspaper and stands up. 'Not today.'

'But you can hardly get in the door,' Nina protests. 'Why don't you let me neaten it up, at least?'

I make my lunch and Daniel's, then bully him out of the door.

'Why are you walking so fast, Jake?' he complains. 'The bus doesn't come for twenty minutes!'

'You won't die because you missed the last few minutes of Ben Ten,' I snap. 'It's like a fridge in there, anyway. I don't want to hang around while they glare at each other behind our backs. I hate it.'

'Do you think she'll really clean out the garage?' Daniel says in a small voice. I know what he's thinking. The boxes of Mum's clothes are in the garage. Neither of us has dared to touch them since Dad carefully taped them shut three years ago.

'No,' I reply. 'Dad won't let her.'

The cold has eased a little with the rising of the sun, but I'm wearing gloves and a beanie as well as my jacket. I'm walking fast to warm up and to put a bit of distance between myself and the house, but as we pass the park I slow down. Most of the trees are European and have lost their leaves, leaving crooked branches bare, like claws. I peer between their trunks, searching for any sign that what I saw last night was real.

'Number forty-seven's watching us again.'

I whirl, just in time to see the lace curtain swing back into place. The back of my neck prickles.

'What's Mrs Henders' problem? Does she think we're going to steal her horrible pink flamingos or something? What are you looking at, anyway – is there something in the park?'

'No.' I reply. 'There's nothing there.'

But even though that's exactly what my eyes tell me, I don't really believe it. And how can I know for sure that it's a dream unless . . .

'Walk to the bus stop by yourself,' I say. 'I've got to do something.'

'What? What are you doing?'

'None of your business. I'll meet you there.'

'Okay.' He shrugs, already a couple of steps ahead of me. I pull out my phone and fiddle with it until he is out of sight, then glance back at our house to make sure Dad or Nina aren't watching. Then I sprint across the road and into the park.

In the morning light things look so different. I spot two people walking along the bike path, but there is no one else around. I walk quickly across to the lake.

When I can't see anything, I tell myself I'm an idiot for thinking I would. And that's when my foot sinks through a piece of charred something. The area in which I stand is bare of grass, and the pieces around the edges are blackened and crushed. Around my feet are black burn-marks, partially frozen over but still visible. These marks have been left by something hot enough to melt through the ice and scorch the mud underneath.

These marks are proof that something happened last night. But what in the world could have made them – and leave behind a living, breathing girl?

And if she does exist, where is she now?

I look around. There are several pieces of flattened grass nearby, frozen in place, but that could have been done by anything in the past few days.

Right, I think. If I was as scared as angel girl was last night, where would I go? I wouldn't want to stay around here. It's too open. But across the lake, on the far bank, the pine plantation extends down to the shore. It is dark and thick, and I know it's a good place to hide.

I jog the distance to keep warm, rounding the lake and ducking through the gap in the two-metre chain-link fence. The pines smell damp, and the clay of the hillside draws the temperature down another five degrees. Pine needles slip under my feet. I climb the hill, heading for a high point where I can see a wider area. Daniel and I built a treehouse here a few years ago, in the tallest pine tree, on the recommendation of Keira, who said you'd be able to see the entire area from up there; down to the park on one side and over the hill to the Garter Street bridge on the other. The treehouse is falling to pieces now; it's just a few rotting wooden boards held in place by rusting nails.

They used to mine sandstone here and the hillside is riddled with caves and tunnels. Daniel and I know them like the back of my hand, even though we've been warned time and time again that such places aren't safe. Would the angel girl have sought shelter in one of them?

I pause. Was that a noise I heard, or just my imagination? The pines creak softly. I am breathing hard from exertion, and I try to calm myself and listen. I keep climbing, but more quietly now, stopping every now and then – and I hear it again, a soft rustling of footsteps.

I don't turn towards the sound. If she is watching me, she would be startled if I did that, and I don't want her to run away again. So I keep climbing, then sidestep behind the thick trunk of a tree and slide back down a little way as quietly as I can. I crouch there, listening.

There is another rustling, then the sound of someone creeping towards where I last stood. I wait until they are closer . . . closer . . . slowly, I peep over the edge of the wall. A figure in a red jacket stares back at me.

'You little shit!' I growl, grabbing Daniel by the collar. 'You followed me.'

'You wouldn't tell me what you were doing!' Daniel protests, yanking himself free. 'What are you doing?'

'I'm looking for insects. It's a science project. You'll miss the bus!'

'So will you,' he reasons. 'And why are you looking for insects here? For starters, it's winter –'

'It's none of your business.' I grind my teeth, resisting the urge to punch him. Instead I grab him by the shirt and drag him back down the hill. We miss the bus, and Nina is silent as she drives us to school.

'You kids have a good day,' she says as we get out of the car. She sounds like a robot.

Chapter 3
Number Forty-Seven

I'M watching Keira when Baz chucks a basketball at my head. 'Sports tryouts are on today.' he grins as I snatch it easily out of the air. 'Ready for the best basketball game you ever played?'

I sneer at him. 'You reckon you even stand a chance?'

'I'll wipe the floor with you, Jake Miles.'

I shake my head, even though he could probably beat me if he was blindfolded, given that I can't seem to concentrate on a single thing today.

'So,' Baz says, flopping down on the grass beside me and leaning in close. 'Keira broke up with Andrew.'

We watch her. She's playing soccer goalie with the same amount of energy she applies to everything else – far too much. She borders on hyperactive even at the worst of times. I wonder if she ever sleeps. Her pony-tail flying out behind her, she tackles the ball in midair and rolls to the ground, coming up grass-stained and yelling in triumph while Mikhal, who'd kicked what he thought would be an easy goal, shakes his head in shame.

'Yeah,' I say.

'So whaddaya reckon?'

'About what?'

'Me and her, dickhead!' Baz rolls his eyes.

I frown. 'You like her?'

Baz rolls his eyes. It's a stupid question. Everyone likes Keira. But in my estimation, no-one likes her as much as me. It's all a complete waste of time – because she always talks to me.

Yeah, I know that should be a good thing, but the problem is that she talks to me as a friend. And that means she doesn't even think about me in the way I think about her.

I'm not sure I like Baz thinking about her that way. Baz hardly knows her, but she used to come and play in our treehouse. She knew the plantation hideouts just as well as Daniel and I did. She had baked biscuits with my mum while I'd hovered around pinching chocolate chips. When Mum got sick, she'd come to the hospital every day with a loaf of fresh bread and a bag of fruit scones. Her mum, Mrs Leichman, worked at the local bakery.

I spin the ball on my finger. 'You know what?' I say. 'I think I'll see if I can get on the soccer team instead.'

Baz looks across at me. 'Good idea!' he says.

I kick myself for mentioning it.

Keira is infectious. Her energy is catching. You even breathe faster when she's around.

'Did you see that save?' she says breathlessly, bouncing over to me at the edge of the oval, brushing her hair back out of her eyes. 'I was like, I'm never going to get it, but it caught my fingers – right here on the tips – and then . . .'

'I saw it,' I say. Yeah, I saw it, right before Mr Alderston lobbed the soccer ball into my face. My nose feels like it's broken, and has turned a shiny red. I look like a clown but Keira doesn't even notice.

We walk back to the change rooms.

'What are you so quiet about?' she says, poking me in the arm hard enough to bruise. 'Miles! Start talking!'

Talking. Again. 'Nothing,' I say.

'They're at it again, aren't they?'

I look at her. 'Who? What?'

'Your dad and Nina, silly. Whatever-she-is.'

'Yeah. I guess.'

'So they're fighting? Not talking? Throwing marshmallows at passing cars?'

'Yeah,' I say. I want to tell her more. I want to say that they smile whenever they catch me or Daniel looking at them. And that when they fight they do it in whispers, thinking that we won't hear them. And that Dad jets off to work whenever he can, and smokes too much, and Nina pulls her lips tight over her teeth and starts tidying the house. I know Keira will understand. She cried more than I did at Mum's funeral.

But suddenly Sharna Devon is there. They appear out of the woodwork, her friends, because they're everywhere. Like flies. And they're off, talking about practice, about the match next week, about talent scouts, and why Mikhal won't ever get the ball past Keira.

***

Dad doesn't ask me if I made the basketball team. I have to tell him I got onto the soccer team instead. His eyebrows crinkle up for a moment, because he's forgotten that I even play sport, I think, but then he nods. 'Oh.' He nods again. 'Good, good. Good.'

'So I thought we could do some practice to-night.'

'Yeah,' he says. 'Yeah, we'll see.'

Which means he'll be on the phone all night.

Nina cooks, and it's pasta again. I chase the soggy stuff around my plate for a while, then say I've got homework to do. I pull out my maths book but keep looking out the window. I can hear the normal evening noises. Dad in the study, talking on the phone. Nina banging around in the kitchen. Daniel's TV show. I'm unnoticed as I grab a torch and creep down the hallway and through the front door.

It's colder than ever, like a slap across the face. I run. The lights from people's living rooms fall over the park, but they only make deeper shadows of the trees. Number forty-seven, though, is dark. No sign of Mrs Henders.

***

I go to the lake. The patch of ash is only a dark stain under my torchlight now – could be anything really. I push through the bushes around the lake, playing the torchlight over the ground. It's so quiet. It's like everyone's gone, like every living thing has suddenly disappeared, and I'm the only person left.

The stars are so bright, so sharp-edged they hurt your eyes. I'm standing on the icy grass, my head craned back to look at them, when she comes.

I don't know where she was hiding, but when I look down she's just there, standing in her white dress, feet bare on the frozen mud, long hair tattered and pale face stained with dirt.

'Are you okay?' I ask her.

She looks at me. I'm not sure if she understands. She moves her head – a nod? A shrug? I try to get a look at her eyes, to see if the pupils are dilated. I don't think they are, but I don't know, there are probably drugs that don't even do that, and she must be on something because it's not right, it's not normal, for anyone to stand there in this weather and not be shivering.

'What's your name?'

She just keeps looking at me. It's almost as if she can't believe what she's seeing, as if she's trying to make sense of me. I shift uncomfortably. 'I'm Miles. Jake, really, Jake Miles. It's . . . it's a nickname.'

She stares.

'Aren't you cold?' My breath is visible in white puffs of vapour. I rub my hands together. 'Cold? I don't know . . . do you speak? Can you speak English? Ah –' Floundering, I wonder if she's German. We had German exchange students at school a few months ago, but they knew a bit of English, even though some of the words were all strangled. They taught us plenty of German swear words, but I'm not sure those are going to be any use right now.

What am I thinking? German? She's not German. She fell out of the sky!

'It's so strange.'

It takes me a moment to realise that she has actually spoken. 'What?'

She doesn't answer. I wonder if she's going to faint or something.

'Do you know where you are?'

She says nothing. But at least I know she speaks English and she understands me. 'You're in Cassidy Heights. Phoenix Park. Um . . . that's Mercer Street up there, towards the Garter Street Bridge, and the highway runs off Juniper Avenue. Just over the next block. Where are you from? Are you lost?'

'I'm . . .' she says softly, her voice a croak. 'Yes. I'm lost.'

'Right.' I nod, trying to be confident. 'Well, tell me where you're from and I'll help you get home. We live across the road. My dad's at home, and Nina. She can drive you wherever you need to go.'

'No.' She shakes her head, and it's a short, sharp shake like a convulsion. 'No, I'm lost.'

'I see,' I say, not understanding at all. 'Well, do you want to come to my house? Dad and Nina can help...'

'No. I can't. I have to . . .' she's looking around now, her eyes darting all over the place. 'I have to . . .'

'It's safe. I'm not going to hurt you or anything, and it's really cold out here. You must be freezing.'

'No. I can't go anywhere. I have to stay. I can't leave.'

'Why?'

She stares, at a loss. If she's been out here since last night, she'll be suffering hypothermia. Maybe it's making her confused.

'Look,' I say. 'I can't make you do anything. But you can trust me. There's a lot of other people around here that you probably can't say the same for.' I'm thinking about crazy old Mrs Henders in number forty-seven, who's probably watching us right now. 'If you really want to stay here, try and find somewhere warm and stay out of sight.'

If she understands, she doesn't show it. Then a sudden noise grabs my attention – Dad, maybe, opening the front door and slipping out for a smoke – and when I turn back she's walking away, quickly, her head down, almost running. The dark shadows swallow her up. I want to go after her, but how can I? She'd think I'm stalking her or something. And whatever is up with her is really none of my business.

I walk slowly back to the road. Number forty-seven's lights are still off, but I catch a glimpse of movement behind the reflections on the window. A surge of anger holds me in place a moment while I glare at the vacated spot. For a moment I just want to march up and bang on the stupid old lady's door and ask her if she doesn't have anything better to do, but that urge is quickly quelled when the front door is wrenched unexpectedly open. I'm caught like a rabbit in the headlights.

She actually isn't all the old, I reckon, but she has one of those faces that's all dragged down by gravity so that her wrinkles sag under her chin, and she's pulled her hair back so tightly it looks like a white swimming cap against her skull. Her eyes are too bright and seem to look right through you. There's something odd about her whole appearance, but I can never work out exactly what it is.

I step away from the gate, putting my head down, ready to run for it.

'Wait.'

It's a command, and it's impossible to do anything except obey. I stop and wait while she walks, moving pretty quickly, down the path between her ugly garden ornaments. All the while she's got her eyes on me. I wonder if she even blinks. This close, I can see the fine workings of her bones beneath her skin. Her voice is soft when she finally speaks.

'You saw, didn't you?'

I shake my head automatically. 'Saw what?'

'Don't give me that,' she hisses. 'You saw. I can tell.'

'I don't know what you're talking about, Mrs Henders,' I reply politely. 'My dad's waiting for me.'

'Don't tell a soul,' she breathes. 'No one can know. You understand that, don't you?'

I back off. I'm already back in front of my own house as she starts to speak, jumping the fence and landing in the garden by the time she's finished the sentence. And I'm back inside, back in my room, the words still ringing in my ears only seconds later. Daniel is pressed against the window. He looks around as I come in.

'What did she say to you?' he asks.

'Nothing,' I say, and ignore his reproachful stare. I feel weird, as if I've forgotten to do something important. Trying to do my homework is useless. All I can see is her, the angel girl. When I go to bed that night I feel guilty for being so warm and comfortable while she is out there – even if she doesn't seem to mind about the cold. I wish she'd let me give her my jacket.

We go to bed but I toss and turn until Daniel rolls over. 'Stoppit,' he murmurs sleepily. 'M'tryina sleep.'

I open my eyes and stare at the dim white shade of the ceiling. What was Mrs Henders on about, anyway? Had she seen the flash, too? I shiver, not at all reassured. After all, that only means that I'm just as crazy as her.

'I can hear you,' says Daniel, exasperated. 'Jus' go to sleep.'

'Sorry,' I say.

Chapter 4
My Friend

KEIRA. If there is one thing that eclipses everything that's tossing around in my head at the moment, it's Keira. She's jigging up and down in her chair, her repressed energy enough to be felt as a physical force. The science teacher has given up yelling at her.

'You know, when it comes down to it,' she's saying now, 'who really gives a crap? If Andrew's going to go around saying all that stuff, then he's obviously not over it, right? So he can just deal with it. It's no one else's problem.'

Baz is sitting next her. 'You're so wise, Keira. You're like Dr Phil.'

'Yeah.' She rolls her eyes. 'Coz you would know.'

'Dr Phil? He's my personal hero. My role model.' He puts on a drawling accent. '"What the hell y'all doin' with yer life?"'

She swats him over the head and turns to me. 'Relationships are just so stupid. How can anyone take themselves seriously if they're mooning around like idiots all day long? Why do you think I broke up with loser-boy?'

'Yeah, he's being a dick about the whole thing.' Of course, I've got no idea what Andrew's been saying about Keira, but I'm rewarded with a satisfied nod of agreement that keeps me flying through the next few minutes. That is, until Mr Jass starts handing out bits of paper and talking about a group project.

'You'll work in pairs,' he says. 'Barry, you and Miss Leichman seem to be hitting it off . . .'

Baz turns and pumps a fist in the air while I resignedly turn to Sharna Devon.

'. . . so I'll pair you with Sharna. Jake, you're with Keira. See if some of your good work ethic rubs off on her? Nigel, with David. Jessica . . .'

I give Keira a small smile that doesn't betray my racing pulse. She grins. 'We'll kick their arses,' she vows. 'You and me, Miles. How can we lose?' A friendly thump on the arm. 'There's no soccer tonight. We'll go to your house after school.'

I'm nodding senselessly and still doing it three hours later as Keira walks with me from the bus stop. Daniel is up ahead, glancing over his shoulder at us. I ignore him.

Outside number forty seven, Keira pauses. 'I remember we used to say she was a witch,' she says. 'I see her taste in garden ornaments hasn't improved.'

I hurry her through our front gate. Maybe she didn't see the curtain twitch, but I did, and I don't relax until we're inside, spreading Tim Tam crumbs all over our textbooks.

'So basically, you want to grow some pot plants,' she says, scrawling notes on the back of the biscuit wrapper. 'Call it an experiment in biodiverstiy if you like, but I reckon it sounds boring as hell, Miles.'

'Yeah.' I have to agree. 'But it'll get us a pass.'

'I don't want to just pass. I want to blow the world away. No, I want to show Jass up. He's a bastard.'

'Yeah,' I say. 'Right.'

She sighs and leans back on the kitchen chair. 'I hate too many people, you know. They just drive me up the wall. I need to be more like you. I need to just stand back and look. But like that thing with Andrew saying all that stuff about me at school? It gets me all worked up, and then I just get mad and everything else goes out the window.'

'I don't stand back and look.' I'm not even sure what she means by that. My stupid fogged-up brain isn't processing anything beyond the fact that a strand of her hair has come loose and is curling around her ear.

'You do. You see things. Stuff other people always miss. You get it, see?' She shakes her head at my uncomprehending look. 'I can't explain it. I shouldn't have to. You live it every day, you should know. Just promise me you won't go and change, right? Not like Andrew, acting like a stupid idiot all of a sudden. I need you to stay like you are forever.'

I laugh. It's a little uncertain. 'Um . . .'

'I'm sick of this.' Standing up, she slams her books closed. 'But keep thinking. We need an angle on this, Miles. I don't want to get sucked into doing just another poster with a Word Art heading. We'll talk more later, right? Call me or something.'

When she's gone, I find Daniel hiding on the stairs. 'She hasn't come round in ages. Why's she coming round now?' he asks.

'We've got a project to do together.'

'You should get her to fix up the treehouse. She was good at hammering nails.'

***

It's later that night, and I'm already awake and looking out the window before I realise it. I'm looking down at the park, at an angle through the trees where I can see something moving just a little bit. It's weird because there's no moon out tonight, so I shouldn't be able to see anything. It stops. It's gone. I sit up and pull my jacket on over my tracksuit.

Into the night. I walk across the road, into the shelter of the trees. Just there, under one of the oaks, she's standing and staring up at the sky. One hand is flat against the bark as if to hold her steady. 'They're gone,' she says softly. She shakes her head, a lost, hopeless gesture.

'Can I help?'

'I don't think so,' she says. 'No. I'm pretty sure you can't. Why do you keep coming back?'

I hesitate. 'I saw you fall the other night. I saw the flash.'

Her eyes are shadowed and I can't tell what she's thinking.

'I'm not going to tell anyone,' I blabber. 'I meant what I said. You can trust me. If you don't want anyone to know you're here, I won't tell them, but you can't just stay here. Sooner or later . . . well, it's not safe.'

'It's never safe.' Her voice is really quiet now, barely audible. 'Not here.'

'What did you mean?'

She sighs. 'I don't think you'd understand.'

'You did fall. I saw it happen.'

I want her to deny it. I want her to laugh and say that's stupid, and only crazy old ladies like Mrs Henders make up stories like that.

She doesn't.

'And things like that don't happen every day. At least, not that I know of. How could I not come back?'

She regards me through the veil of shadows.

'You don't have to tell me anything. Just let me get you some food and a blanket. Please.'

A silence, longer this time, as she turns her gaze back to the sky. She does speak, but not for a while. 'I was talking about the stars. The stars are gone.'

'It's only clouds,' I assure her. 'The stars are still there, you just can't see them.'

'I really, really wish I could see them.'

I stare at her. 'Look, I can't stay out here all night. My brother will wake up and notice I'm gone. If you want me to bring you some food, well, I will. Or clothes or anything. Just let me know.'

'I am hungry,' she says slowly.

Grinning, I offer my hand, then hastily withdraw it when I realise what I'm doing. 'Come with me,' I say instead.

And she does.

Chapter 5
The Gift

AT night, spaces are warped. Everything looks different. I turn the light on in the kitchen, but it doesn't chase away the strange sense of being awake while the rest of the world is asleep. I pull out a chair and she sits down tentatively – she moves like a cat, warily looking around, tensed and ready to spring for the door. Her eyes are wide as she takes in the fridge, the bench covered in dishes, the microwave, the rubbish bin. She looks like she's never seen anything like them.

'There's not much to choose from,' I say, pulling a bottle of juice out of the fridge, and some leftover pizza. I pour the juice into a glass, and she looks at the pizza cautiously.

'It smells bad,' she says.

I frown. 'It's fine. We ordered it for tea. Only a couple of hours ago.'

'No.' She shakes her head. 'It smells of dead things.'

'It's got ham on it.'

'Is that something that died?'

'Yeah, I guess. Ham used to be pigs.' Her expression stops my laughter. It's as if I just told her that she'd have to eat vomit. 'Are you vegetarian?'

'I don't know what that is.' She's perplexed.

'Well, there's not much else – um, oh, there's this. Garlic bread. Daniel hates it so there's tons left.' I pull off the foil and put it in the microwave. The girl watches carefully as it lights up and the plate starts to revolve.

The microwave beeps, and I pull the plate out and set it in front of her. She falls on it, tearing off a bit and cramming it in her mouth. It's painful to watch. 'It tastes . . .' she frowns.

'You don't like it?'

'No. It's good.'

As if to prove it, she devours the rest in under a minute. I pour her some more juice, and manage to find a can of peaches, which she inhales as well. I wouldn't have thought it the most appetising combination, but she doesn't complain.

'I've always wondered about these wrappers. All the food here comes packaged and labelled,' she says, toying with the empty can.

'Well, yeah. The packaging makes it last longer. And helps you pick which brand you want.'

'Thank you for the meal,' she replies politely.

'Don't go back to the park,' I plead. 'We've got a garage. No one ever goes in there. It's only full of boxes of . . .' I pause, thinking about exactly what the garage is full of – the cardboard boxes that Dad taped shut so carefully, as if by sealing them tightly enough, he could keep his memories of Mum inside them, safe for years to come. 'Well, full of old stuff.'

She shakes her head. She won't stay. 'I need to be in the park,' she says. 'Just in case.'

'Well, at least I can give you something warm to wear.' I go through the door into the laundry. Thank goodness for Nina's charitable urges – the bags we filled for the Salvo's winter appeal are in the corner. I pick out one of Daniel's old jackets and a thick woollen blanket. 'You can take these with you.'

She nods her head. 'Thank you.'

'Be careful. Don't let anyone see you.'

The door is closed, and she is gone into the swirling ice-mist of early morning.

Back in bed, I barely sleep at all. When Nina gets Daniel up, she wakes me as well, but she's working and leaves early. I fall back to sleep, only to wake up at eight-thirty and realise I've got ten minutes to shower, get dressed, pack my bag and get to the bus stop.

I'm walking bleary-eyed past number forty-seven when Mrs Henders looms up in front of me.

'You be careful,' she croaks.

'I'm really late,' I say, moving to step past her. Quick as a flash, she grabs my arm, her bony fingers digging in like sharp claws.

'You've got to be careful,' she says, and she shoves something at me.

'What is this?'

She smirks. 'Something I made. Something you'll need.'

Suddenly the hand is gone, and she's shambling back up the path as if nothing happened. I'm left holding the whatever-it-is. It's wrapped in brown felt. Slowly, carefully, I let it unfold in my hands. Inside is a tube of dark metal – it looks like brass, which explains the weight. It's an old fashioned telescope, tarnished with age.

What the hell?

I turn it over in my hands, shaking my head. And then I remember I'm late for the bus, and I shove it into my pocket and sprint like hell.

***

'Hey Miles!' Baz grabs me from behind in a strangle-hold. I shake him off. In my pocket, the telescope shifts, and I grab it to make sure it doesn't fall out.

'What?'

'You missed soccer last night.'

I realise it's true. I'd completely forgotten about practice.

'You missed the action,' he goes on.

'What?'

'What do you think?' At my blank look, he sighs impatiently. 'Where's your head today? I'm talking about Keira, numbnuts!'

'What about her?'

He rolls his eyes. 'She was practically begging me to ask her out, yesterday.'

'She said relationships were for idiots.'

'She's going out with me!'

Ice-crystals form in my veins. I can feel them pricking my heart. 'She's going out with you?'

He's already bouncing down the hallway.

I get through homeroom, maths, and history, but when it comes to recess I'm ready to collapse. I want to crawl back into bed and pretend that this day never happened.

Baz is playing no-rules footy with some of the other guys in the hallway, bouncing the ball off light-fittings and people's heads, and I can't even look at him without feeling like I'm going to throw up, so I grab my jacket and sit outside near the library and pretend to eat my lunch. It tastes like crap so I end up just sitting there, and when Keira plonks herself down next to me, I jump.

'What's up?'

I'm about ready to throw up again. 'Nothin'.'

'Bull.'

She can say whatever she wants, but I'm not talking.

'You up for the movies on Friday? That new one – The Witch.'

I shrug. It's all about some gruesome murder,

which really suits my mood right now, but honestly . . .

'Well, we're all going.'

'Baz too?' It just slips out, and she kind of stiffens up. Not that I'm watching, I'm too busy studying the remains of my salad roll spread out on my lap.

'Yeah,' she says. 'Yeah, I guess you heard.' She's smiling a little bit, at the corners of her mouth. 'You know, I never reckoned he would ask me out, but he walked me home from soccer practice and he was so sweet.'

'Right.' Really, I don't want to hear it.

'And yeah. It's a good thing. Right?'

'What you said, yesterday, when you were talking about Andrew,' I remind her.

'I only said people who act like him should be shot. Baz isn't like that. It's good. It's like we're still best mates.'

I feel things shift around in my stomach. Ugh. 'I think I want to work on our project on Friday.'

'Really?' She sounds really surprised. 'Well, okay, Miles. Don't expect me to hang with you, though. I'm busting to go out, so I'll let you do the homework-obsessed loner thing, okay?'

'No worries,' I say. 'See you.'

I'm in such a bad mood I wag the last two periods and walk home. But when I reach my house I don't go inside. I cross the road into the park.

Sitting on the bench by the pond, I take out the telescope. The metal is so cold it burns me.

I rub my fingers over the worn surface, but it doesn't warm up with my body heat.

Crazy Mrs Henders. Why, out of all the people she probably spies on, does she have to pick on me to talk to?

I pull out the extendable sections. They're stiff and I have to twist them to get them to move. The eyepiece is ice-cold when I put it to my eye. The view it shows me is nothing remarkable – the glass is smudged and scarred with scratches. I can see the faint shapes of two joggers. Strangely, they're both surrounded by a shifting turquoise cloud. The trees on the far side of the pond look blurred and out-of-focus, and they're all surrounded by a faint red haze.

It's weird. They don't look any closer, but there's a definite rose tinge clinging to the trunks and branches. When I move the telescope higher, the haze turns to a soft orange. I guess the glass must be tinted or have filters or something in it that have discoloured over time.

When I shift the telescope to the side a little, I catch sight of a thin yellow line. It stops short of touching the tops of the trees. At first I think it's a vapour trail from an aeroplane, but it's too thin and straight.

I lift the telescope, tracing the line upwards. But the sky that should have been there . . . isn't there.

This fact registers calmly in my mind, as if someone had just told me that their favourite band was *Good Charlotte*. I'm looking up at what should have been the clouds, but I'm seeing clear blue sky instead, shot through with bright little pinprick stars. The yellow streak reaches up and vanishes. Right there, hanging before my eyes, it's . . . it's unimaginable. Spires and turrets, the tallest towers stretching up impossibly high. Bridges span the distances between them, tiny slender things like strands of a spider's web. In the light of late evening, against the backdrop of stars, it shines silver. It's a city. It's a city in the sky.

It's a city.

Slowly, very slowly, I remove the telescope from my eye. The clouds are back. There is nothing, not a trace to show how this could have happened, how this illusion could have been performed. I shake the telescope. Almost reluctantly, I replace it against my eye. The city shimmers into being.

I am insane.

Suddenly not wanting to touch the thing anymore, I tuck the telescope into my backpack. I'm only sitting there for about three minutes before she shows up, walking across the grass. She looks odd, holding a folded blanket and wearing Daniel's old jacket over her white dress, but though it doesn't really disguise the strangeness about her I'm glad that she looks less . . . remarkable.

'You look pale,' she says.

She looks really concerned, and for a moment I'm just going to sit here and lap it up. People should be concerned! For a moment I get the urge to tell her everything, about Keira and Baz, about Mrs Henders, about what I just saw in the sky. She won't laugh. She won't call me insane. She'll listen carefully and nod and look at me with those deep blue eyes.

But I don't. I don't want to talk about any of it. Grasping for normality I give her the answer I would give Dad or Nina – a shrug. 'I'm fine. Just school stuff.'

'Oh,' she says.

'But what about you? Are you warmer?'

'Yes. I've never been cold, ever, before I came here. But this place is so different. I can't quite work things out.' She shakes her head. 'You're purple,' she says, and then shakes her head, frustrated, when she sees I'm confused. 'Upset, and sad. I'm curious – school is a place you go to learn about history and writing?'

I give a little snort, because I think she's joking. But she's not. She just looks at me and I have to tell her. 'School is pretty much about everything but learning. How can you not know about school?' Where in the world is there a place that kids don't go to school? Is she from Africa or some third world country? Surely not with that pale skin . . . I'm doing it again. She's not from Africa, or Germany, I tell myself. Angel girl is not from here at all.

'I do,' she says. 'I know some things. I've watched it sometimes.'

'That doesn't make any sense.' I sigh. 'I said I wouldn't ask you questions, so I won't ask where you're from again. But I'd really like to know.'

She smiles slightly. 'Did you do badly? In one of your history or writing lessons?'

'No.' I'm short with her this time. I'm respecting her privacy, even though it's killing me. Why can't she do me the same courtesy? 'I'll get you some food. Oh, wait. Come with me. Nina will be home, but that doesn't matter.'

She looks wary. 'I'm not all that hungry.'

'You have to eat,' I tell her. 'Come on. Nina's probably done some shopping.'

We walk out of the park. I glance at number forty-seven. Even though there's no movement behind the curtains, I reckon she's watching us. I feel the weight of the telescope in my pocket – I'll have to hide it somewhere later, so that Daniel doesn't find it. I feel like I've got a million secrets!

'You're early,' says Nina. She's in the kitchen, bills spread out on the table in front of her, and she looks up when we come in. She looks a bit startled to see us. I wonder if she'll recognise Daniel's old jacket, but she doesn't seem to notice. 'Oh. Hello.'

'This is Rebecca,' I cover quickly. 'From my class. We're doing homework.'

'Hi, Rebecca. I'm Nina.'

Oh, I hate that so much, that suck-up 'I'm the coolest adult ever' look she gets on her face every time she meets one of our friends. I grit my teeth and bear it. I don't want to start arguing with her.

'Do you want Milo? There's some biscuits in the cupboard. Or bread – there's jam, or Nutella.'

'Thanks,' I say. I'm already getting out the milk and mugs.

'Are you working on the science project too?' Nina asks.

I get a panicked look.

'No. She's in a different group. They're doing animal migration patterns.' To tell you the truth, I'm a bit surprised at how easily all these lies are coming out.

'Well, if you need any help with that, one of my friends works for the EPA – she could probably give you some pretty good information . . .'

'Thanks, but we're all supposed to do the research ourselves.'

I'm not waiting for milk to warm up – I chuck the Milo in cold, grab some biscuits and lead the way out from under Nina's eager gaze.

In the bedroom, she sits on the edge of Daniel's bed like she's going to get up and bolt at a moment's notice. She takes a tentative sip of Milo and her eyes light up. 'It tastes wonderful. Like spices and sweetness.'

I raise my eyebrows.

'This is where you sleep?' she goes on, her eyes roving over the room.

'Yes. That's my brother's bed.'

She nods. 'You have a brother?'

'Yeah. He's a pain.'

'You don't like him?'

'Does anyone like their siblings?' I shake my head. 'He's not too bad, as brothers go. He's a lot like me though, and I don't know – I don't know if that's a good thing.' I want to ask her if she's got any brothers or sisters, but I promised I wouldn't pry. But in the next instant, she's answered my question for me.

'I'd like it,' she says. 'I think I would. If I had a brother. I've seen brothers and sisters together here. I'd like to have someone I was that close to.'

It's the most she's ever said at one time. I'm kind of shocked. 'Well, if you want to take him, go ahead.'

A moment, just a moment, and I think I can see the faintest trace of a smile on her lips. It takes hold tentatively, like she's used to laughing out aloud but hasn't done it in a very long time. 'What's his name?'

'Daniel.' I finish my Milo. 'And I'm Jake. Jake Miles. Remember, I told you?'

She nods. 'I remember you, Jake Miles.'

For a moment I think she's going to tell me her own name, but no such luck – she seems to realise what she's doing and she's sitting up straight again, her eyes darting around. I can almost see her folding in on herself.

'That's Nina, who you met in the kitchen. And my dad – Alex – he's at work. He always is.'

'Does he like being at work?'

'I don't know. I don't think so. I think he just likes not being here.'

'I would like to work,' she says. 'If I could.'

'Work at what?' And why? Work doesn't seem particularly appealing to me. Look at how it makes Dad act, the way he gets all cut up about things, and comes home silent, and locks himself in his study for hours without talking to anyone and if one of us makes a noise he'll come out and yell like anything. And Nina, well, her job doing part-time accounting just sounds boring. 'You don't go to school, right? So you've got plenty of free time. Why can't you work?'

'It's . . . hard to explain. Things are very different where I come from. When I was little, I always wanted to be a . . . a healer.'

I frown. 'Like a doctor.'

She brightens a moment. 'Yes! A doctor. It's all I wanted to do.'

'So why don't you? You can get a casual job and save up, then go to uni . . .' even as I speak the words, I know I'm saying the wrong thing. Casual job. Uni. They're words that she doesn't know, concepts that don't apply to her.

'Here, that is what you would do. But in my place it is very different. People have their roles to fulfil and choice does not come into it. And now . . .' Here she pauses for a long moment, her face going oddly still. I might be imagining that there are tears in her eyes, but I see her lower lip quiver.

'Now?'

'I don't know.' Her voice lowers to a whisper. 'I don't even know if I can ever go home.'

'Don't cry,' I say, embarrassed because she says this with such sadness that I think it's going to make me start bawling.

'I'm not,' she says it as if she truly believes that she's not. She puts her empty cup on the floor and stands up, moving towards the door, making her escape.

'No —' I start after her. I really don't want her to leave, not now, when she's actually talking to me and I'm close to discovering who she is. I can't let her. I grab her arm to stop her, and in that instant I'm —

I'm —

I am.

I'm here, I'm not, I'm nothing compared to the everything I've become. Suddenly I am part of the wind outside the window, the noise of the TV in the lounge room, the minute vibrations of the house as wood and brick and plaster shifts infinitesimally. I can see at once Daniel's Ben Ten poster on the wall and Nina downstairs, still sitting at the table and staring blankly at the bills spread out in front of her, and a jogger in the park and a bird flying towards a red rooftop and my own hand gripping her arm. But not only this, I feel them — the crispness of the paper and the rush of air against feathered wings and the thud of the earth beneath the joggers feet and the echoing click of Nina's fingernails on the Laminex.

I can't think of any other way to describe it. It's like it's all there − no, it's always been there, but now I realise how much a part of it I am, and how much everything is a part of everything else. It's all linked, from the tiniest molecule of air to the sound of traffic on the distant highway, from the smell of Milo to the feel of her ice cold skin under my fingers. I let go, and with a jolt, I am dumped back into my body. Her arm falls to her side and she looks at me and I see in her midnight eyes horror and fear. She backs away from me. 'You shouldn't have done that.'

'I'm sorry,' I apologise uselessly, dizzy from the shock of it all. I put my hand against the wall to feel something solid because the world is rocking. It's just like that first time I touched her, in the park, just after she fell − but it's a thousand times worse. I feel like I'm going to throw up.

She turns, and bolts down the hall. I can't go after her. I kneel down and put my forehead on the floor, the carpet pressing deep into my skin, which feels suddenly too hot, too tight. I kind of scrunch myself up into a little ball of pathetic human flesh, a waste of space, a waste of energy and breath.

'Are you okay?'

It's Daniel, Daniel's voice, but it's like a tonne of rocks falling down a mountainside, a piece of sandpaper being forced through my eardrum. I moan, hoping he'll understand, somehow, but of course he's chewing on a muesli bar – I can hear his teeth grinding away at the little grains, splitting them open – and he's full of after-school energy. 'Who's that?'

I roll out of the doorway, prop myself against the wall, and push the heel of my hand into my temple as if that will help.

'Jake? Jake? Who was that?'

'No one,' I mutter.

'What's wrong with you? You look sick. Who was that girl? She was wearing my jacket.'

'You gave that jacket away to the Salvo's.' I'm not really listening to what I'm saying. 'It's not yours anymore.'

He purses his lips, takes another slow, noisy bite of his muesli bar and crinkles the wrapper up in his hands. 'Why doesn't she have her own clothes?'

'Because some people just don't,' I return. 'Which is why you gave away your jacket in the first place. And you can't choose who gets stuff you throw away. That's just stupid.'

'You're stupid!' he retorts. 'You look really sick. I'll get Nina.'

'No!' I yell. He jumps a bit. I'm startled by the way that comes out, too. 'No, I don't want her to know, Daniel. I just got a headache. I'll be fine in a bit. I already feel better.'

It's true. Things are fading, falling back into place. My ears are still ringing, but the sounds have diminished. I still feel nauseous, but I think I can choke it down. I tuck the telescope under my pillow and by tea-time, I'm feeling normal enough to snap at Nina when she goes on about the girl.

'Rebecca seems nice,' she says. 'A bit quiet.'

I shrug, knowing that she's comparing her to my other friends. To Baz. And Keira. Of course, I know what she's thinking. That I'm being a moody teenager and going through 'a stage', or whatever adults call it when you're younger than they are and they don't understand you. I don't know why, because honestly, the way she and Dad carry on, you'd think they were the ones going through a stage.

'She doesn't look like a Rebecca,' Daniel says.

I glare at him.

'She doesn't! It doesn't suit her.'

Nina intervenes. 'You should have told her to stay for tea.'

'She had to get home.'

'Well, you should invite her around some other time, then. We'll have lamb or something. A roast.'

I think about the angel girl's reaction to pizza. 'She's vegetarian. Is Dad going to be late?'

'He's always late,' says Daniel.

'About eleven. Don't wait up for him – he went in at four this morning so he'll probably just go straight to bed. You know.'

Yeah. I know. I guess asking him to help me work on my soccer kicks is out of the question, again.

'And anyway, you could use an early night, I think, Jake. You look a bit peaky.'

For once, I accede, allowing her to bully me into bed with another cup of Milo, hot this time. As the steam curls up past my face, she sits down on the edge of the bed. 'He's just busy, you know. It's hard work.'

'Everything's hard work.'

'But it's harder for some people.' She sighs. 'Look, don't worry about it, okay? He's up for a promotion soon. A higher pay rate means he'll be able to spend less time at the office.'

'Or even more.'

She frowns. 'Don't speak like that. If you had any idea . . .'

'Sorry,' I mumble.

She sighs. 'No you're not. I remember what it was like. I was fifteen too, and my parents were never around. I was selfish and I hated them because there were all these things happening in my own life that were difficult, and then I felt guilty for hating them because I never would have talked to them about it anyway.'

I wonder if I'm supposed to feel sorry for her. I don't. I'm too tired.

'I'm not saying life is more complicated when you're an adult than when you're a kid, but the problems are proportional, you know? And they affect more people because there's a hell of a lot more responsibility involved. I know it's hard being fifteen, but it's not easy being forty-one either.'

She pats at my bedcover, stands up. 'Good night, Jake.'

I don't answer her. The Milo tastes far too sweet and the heat of it burns the roof of my mouth.

Later, I turn over in my sleep. Before I even know I'm doing it, I grab the telescope from beside my pillow, where it's wedged against the wall. I sit up and, taking a deep breath, I look through the window.

It's there, that strange glowing rope trailing up to the sky. The city is brighter now in the darkness. It glitters. I crouch down so that I can see more of it.

The sight of it makes me gasp. My eyes, still sore from the evening's assault on my senses, hurt to see something so bright. I see the towers, the bridges, the beautiful splendour of it all. It's magnificent.

I suddenly wonder about Mrs Henders. Where did she get the telescope from? There's only one reason why she would give it to me. She knows about the city.

Chapter 6
Shar

IT'S Friday.

I've never hated a Friday so much in my life. Usually when the bell rings at the end of the day, Baz and I will be on our bikes heading for the skate park or the cross-country track, or going over to his place to spend a couple of hours on the XBOX. I even ride my bike to school out of habit. But when I slam my locker at the end of the day I catch sight of him, up against the wall with Keira, her fingers in his hair and his tongue jammed firmly between her lips. It's disgusting.

I turn away, heaving my backpack higher and head for the bike racks.

'Miles. Hey, MILES!'

Baz jumps on my back. Overloaded with books I stumble and nearly fall over. Two of my science books fall out of my bag. 'Off me, would you?' I growl.

He has no clue. He's grinning like a maniac. 'The movies, man! You coming?'

'No.'

It's Keira who answers for me, my science books in her hands. 'Miles has decided to spend the night with his good friend the science textbook.'

'Miles,' says Baz, eyes widening in pretend shock.

'I've got work to do,' I say, grabbing my books and shove them back in my bag.

'Yeah, right.' He rolls his eyes. I don't care, I'm already outside and heading for the bike racks. But he comes after me, catching me as I'm undoing the chain. 'Hey,' he says, quieter now and looking over his shoulder at Keira, who's talking to one of her friends over near the taps. 'What's your problem, man?'

'Nothing,' I say innocently. The last thing I want to do is fight right now. Actually, the only thing I want to do is fight, punch him in his stupid grinning mouth. Why can't he just back off?

'Don't give me that. You've been really shitty the past few days. You haven't even been to soccer practice once. Mr Alderston'll kick you off the team.'

He just doesn't get it. He doesn't even understand. How can Keira want him? How can she want him more than me?

Baz doesn't get serious very often, and it's always weird when he does. 'If something's wrong, just tell me what it is.'

'Get out of my way.'

I nearly ram my bike through his leg when he

doesn't move. I want to yell, I want to scream at him. Last night I saw eternity. You'll never see anything as cool as that, will you? And you'll never realise that in the scheme of things like that, we – you, Keira, me – are nothing!

'Fine, whatever it is, figure it out and get over it, okay?' He turns and walks away. Keira, waving to her friend, walks over to him. He says something, shakes his head, and then they're gone, disappearing into the sea of dispersing students.

Fuck him.

***

I ride home. It's a long way, and by the time I get onto my street I'm sweating in the ice-cold air and my bag of science books feels like it weighs a hundred tonnes. I'm at my gate when I see her, the angel girl. She's watching me from across the road, standing by a tree where she can't be seen easily. I guess my efforts at cautioning her haven't been in vain.

I dump my bike and bag on the lawn and cross over the road. I feel a bit wary. After what happened last night, I'm not sure I want to get close to her. Not sure I'm ready to have that happen again. I'm ruffled when I see the same expression reflected in her eyes.

It's a few minutes before I speak. I think she knows what I'm going to say, because she cuts me off before I can form a word. 'It's not supposed to happen,' she says. 'I didn't mean for it to happen.'

Her eyes are locked on mine. Is she apologising?

'I know I said I wouldn't ask you any more questions,' I say. 'But something happened to me when I touched you and I'd really like to know what it was.'

She's still looking at me, so closely, so intensely with those blue eyes. It's a bit hard to breathe with them pressing in on me like that. 'It's called ihlwarh,' she says. 'And it's not supposed to happen. Ihlwarh is a joining of minds. What you saw was a . . . a representation . . . of mine. I think. Where I come from, this joining is as normal as a greeting. But I think it works differently with people like you.'

'People like me? You mean people my age? Gender? Race?' I pause. Meeting her stare. 'You're not talking about race here, are you?'

She shakes her head, slowly.

'I see.' It's all I can think to say.

'For your mind, it must have been an experience.'

I give a little laugh, high-pitched, strangled.

'I'm sorry. It was my fault. I haven't been guarding myself as I should. I let down my barriers because I just hoped . . .' she pauses, looks up at the sky. 'I hoped that I might hear something.'

'Hear something from the city up there?' I say it because I'm half hoping that she'll tell me I'm crazy. Then I could just forget about the whole thing.

For a moment, when her eyes widen and she gives a little gasp, I think maybe she will; but she breathes: 'You've seen it.' Her voice is soft, her eyes pleading. 'But how? It's not supposed to be seen . . .'

'By people like me,' I say, challenging her.

Her eyes narrow and she lifts her jaw. Accepting the challenge. 'Yes.'

I nod. 'You have to tell me what you mean. I think it's important that I know. I said I wouldn't pry, so let's make this an exchange — my secrets for yours.'

'You do not . . .' she starts, then shakes her head. She seems to gather herself, then begins again. 'Tell me how you can see the city.'

'No.' Firmly. 'That's not the way a trade works. I've already told you stuff. I've already given you clothes and food. It's my turn first.'

She swallows, suddenly defensive again.

'What's your name?'

Startled, she puts a hand to her chest. Like she's trying to keep it inside. After a moment, she says it aloud, reluctantly. 'Cari.'

I nod. It suits her better than Rebecca. 'And how old are you?'

'I'm not sure.'

I snap. 'If you're not going to play fair, I'll just go!'

'Be quiet!' she says fiercely. 'Just be quiet! Your time is different and I don't know! Physical age is not important for us. We measure age by experience and ability, not days. How old are you?'

'Fifteen,' I say.

'Tell me how you can see the city.'

'No!' I return. I'm mad and I want to walk away, but how can I? I'm trapped by my own curiosity, by my need to know more about her. 'No. I want more than your name before I trade you that.'

She glares at me.

'I saw you fall from the sky,' I go on. 'I want to know what it is that's going on. I've got a right to know!'

We stand there like that for ages, neither one wanting to back down.

'Fine,' she says at last, turning away. 'You can leave.'

I sigh in frustration. Digging deep into my pocket, I pull out the telescope wrapped in its little square of felt. I shove it at her.

She takes it with gentle hands, unwraps it carefully. She holds the metal tube as if it's the most precious thing in the world. 'Oh,' she says.

I watch her.

She carefully extends it and puts it to her eye. For a long while she gazes at the sky, then slowly she lowers it and turns to me. I can see bleak desperation in her eyes.

When I see her so distressed, my earlier anger is gone in an instant. 'When I look through it, I can see faint colours coming out of things. There's a golden thread reaching up from just above the trees there. And when I point it to the sky, I can see a city. Is that what you see?'

She nods. Reluctantly, she hands it back.

'Even though I'm here, I can still see the colours, on people, and plants. All living things. I suppose it isn't normal in your world to be able to tell how someone is feeling and what they are thinking by their auras, but this telescope lets you see them. Where did you get such a treasure?'

I shrug. 'This insane old woman who lives next door to us gave it to me. She said she made it, and I think she saw you fall the other night, too. So I'm not the only one who knows about the city.'

'There are stories of people who have crossed over from my world to yours – by accident or otherwise. And some from your world have come to mine. But they are carefully isolated. We never hear what happens to them.'

I feel something click into place. Mrs Henders' strangeness – well, it would make sense if – if she knew about the city because she was from . . .

But she's been here for years. She's lived next door to us for ages, peering out from behind her curtains, growling at us when we lose our cricket balls over her fence, yelling at dogs that pee on her fence, adding awful garden ornaments to her collection. Can she really be from Cari's glittering city?

'The city's name,' Cari says, sinking to a crouch with her back against the tree trunk, 'is Shar.'

'How long has it been there?'

There's something childish about the way she says this, as if it was a stupid question. 'It's Shar. The First City and the Last. Until everything else is gone, it will always be there.'

It's not the cold that makes me shiver. 'Then it's like a parallel world.'

'I don't know that term,' she tells me. 'Shar touches your world. It sits alongside it, separated by a boundary. There are bridges which cross this boundary, but they are hard to find, and difficult to cross. Sometimes it is only a one-way journey, and people never find their way back. Shar is my home.'

'What happened to you?'

'I . . . got lost.' she shakes her head. 'No. I'm lying now. Only because I don't want you to think badly of me. And I don't know why I care. I hardly know you.'

'Whatever you did couldn't have been that bad.'

'I didn't say I did anything!'

No, she didn't say that, but it's pretty obvious. What's she hiding?

She sighs. 'It's my turn. Tell me about school. About the anger and hurt that makes you so purple.'

I give a little laugh. 'School? I don't care about school.'

'You do care. I told you, I can see how you feel about it.'

'I don't give a crap what anyone does in that stupid place. I don't care about Keira or Baz. They can both go to hell.'

'Keira and Baz – they are your friends?'

'They were. Maybe. Maybe they weren't, really. It doesn't matter. They all decided to go to the movies tonight and I had a fight with them. Now I'm stuck at home doing homework.'

'You're hurting yourself,' she says quietly.

'What?'

'You're pulling pain in on yourself. Making it worse. It doesn't work when you try to do it like that. Doesn't fix anything.'

'Well, then, what would you suggest?'

She smiles. 'I have never been to see a movie.'

I laugh.

Chapter 7
Shadows

NINA isn't home yet, so I tell Cari that she can have a shower if she wants. She just stares at me, and I realise she has no idea what I'm talking about, so I push her into the bathroom. 'This tap is hot water – well, when the water heater decides to work, it's hot – this one cold. This is soap, and shampoo. Shampoo is for your hair.'

I laugh when she looks at the bottles in bafflement.

'I have seen these things,' she says. 'But I don't understand them.'

'It's for getting your skin and hair clean. You have to squeeze it out, like this, and rub it in, then you wash it off with the water.'

She takes the bottles from me warily.

'You have to undress, first.' When I realise what I've said, I blush horribly and back out of the room.

I wonder about clothes. The Salvo's bags are long gone. I can't pinch any of Nina's good stuff – she didn't notice Daniel's jacket, but if her own clothes go missing, she'll know straight away. I don't have anything small enough to fit her. But then I remember the garage.

***

Nina's right. The garage is a mess. I climb in behind Daniel's old bike and the lawnmower. I push aside an old TV that only gets one channel to uncover the pile of squashed and battered cardboard boxes.

Opening the first, I smell that musty scent clothes get when they're packed away for ages, and a whiff of that faint perfume that Mum used to wear. It's ingrained in everything she owned. I run my fingers through the soft fabrics, familiar patterns grabbing my attention.

I remember the cardigan with the little pink roses. She was wearing it when we went on holiday to Warrnambool that time — there's a photo of us in one of our family albums, with her holding her hair back against the wind, and me crouching down in the sand picking at a half-buried shell, and Daniel walking the other way, his back to the camera. And the blouse she got for her graduation dinner from that business course she did, but she didn't end up wearing it — she wore her blue dress instead because she said she felt like a white collar toff in the starchy shirt.

Jeans and t-shirts. Jumpers and jackets. I pick out some slip-on shoes that look to be the right size, a cream-coloured top, a skirt and a blue jacket – they're plain and could easily be anyone's. I shake the clothes out, then dunk them in hot water and chuck them in the dryer to try and get the musty smell out.

A few minutes later I yell through the bathroom door. 'I'm leaving some clean clothes outside the door.' and then, 'Oh! Use a towel to dry yourself before you get dressed. There's a clean one on the rack – it's blue.'

In my room, I flick through my science book for ideas. Biology – we could grow some plants. Ferns, indoor things that won't get bitten by the frost and die. Or chemistry – cabbage dye acidity indicators or something. Like Keira said, it's all incredibly boring.

The angel girl appears in the doorway. Cari. I remind myself that she has a name now. She's uncertain, looking down at herself, at the strange new clothes. Her hair is damp and hanging in rat-tails. Her skin looks like porcelain, handcrafted and freshly painted.

'Come on,' I say at last. 'I'll show you how to brush your hair.'

***

Nina is overjoyed at the idea of cooking dinner for Rebecca, but I dash her hopes by telling her we're going to be late for the movie. She gives me money for the tickets. I take the rest of my pocket money and we head down our street, turning left on the main road and going across the bridge. Below, the river is caked with ice at its edges. It's already getting dark by the time we reach the mall.

'This place is full of shadows,' says Cari.

'Shadows?'

'There're all these lights,' she says as she points to the bright window displays. 'Everywhere. Like you're trying to shut it out, the night. But you see? It makes it darker.'

It's true. The alleyways, the side streets, underneath cars, everywhere the lights aren't shining, are pitch black. I wonder why I never noticed it before.

'And you can't see the stars,' I say. We both look up then, at the blank sheen of night sky.

'Miiiiiiiillles!'

I turn, and Mikhal punches me in the shoulder. 'Hey.' He's looking past me. At Cari. And smiling.

'You got yourself a friend?'

'Rebecca,' I say. 'This is Mikhal. From school.'

'Rebecca,' he says, and does a deep bow. 'The honour is mine.'

Cari looks at him, wary as a cat, ready to turn around and run at a moment's notice.

Mikhal spots the others across the road. 'BAZZER!' And he's off, bouncing through the evening traffic. I follow more slowly.

'If you want to leave,' I say quietly to Cari, 'just tell me.' Actually, now that we're here, all I want to do is go home.

But her eyes are shining in the flickering lights of the theatre. She shakes her head, and I realise that she's leading me now. Right up to Mikhal, Baz and Keira, who are talking, heads close together, breath steaming in the cold air. Keira's hair is loose. She brushes it back from her face and turns a little to see me. A strange expression crosses her face. But Baz says something, and she laughs, and he puts his hand on her shoulder and I nearly explode. I sidestep Mikhal as he does a flying leap onto the banister and nearly falls on his face when the ice skids him along, and shout g'day to James who's just stepped out of his dad's car, and let everyone look at Cari. I ignore Keira, even when, as we're going inside, she steps up beside me.

I think she was going to say something, but she doesn't.

We buy popcorn and cokes and Malteasers, and Mikhal gets threatened by a security guard when he starts seeing if he can hit the fake chandeliers with them. But I'm watching Cari. Under the glittering lights, she seems to come alive. It's warm enough to take off our jackets, and in the shirt and skirt she looks smaller, her pale skin paler. She's delicate, like an elf. When she moves she makes everyone else look clumsy. She smiles, and it changes her. People are watching. Not just Baz, not just Mikhal and

James, but everyone. I bask in her reflected radiance. She's mine, and I'm showing her off. It's fun.

In the theatre, Baz and Keira sit in the row behind us so they can throw popcorn and kick our seats. I'm too busy watching Cari's face. She stares at the screen with an expression of rapture, so engrossed that she jumps a little when the pistol is fired at the unsuspecting protagonist. It's like watching a little kid. I get kind of wrapped up in her own experience of the movie and even though plot is hashed together out of old horror scripts, it's the best movie I've seen in ages.

Afterwards we head back out into the dazzlingly bright street. Cari's pale skin is luminescent, her blonde hair shining gold. She laughs at James's imitation of the swaggering bad guy. She says her favourite character is the bad guy's friend. 'He's not really bad. He's doing what he thinks is the right thing to do.'

I'm surprised when I find Keira at my elbow. We're standing on the edge of the group, and she touches my arm slightly. 'I'm glad you decided to show up,' she says.

I shrug. 'We were bored.' Cool, calm, collected – I am all of these. Never mind the red-hot spikes of anger stabbing through underneath it all.

'I thought you were studying.'

The anger rises. 'I was bored with studying. Bec came round, and we figured we'd go out for a bit.'

'She's nice.'

Victory. It tastes like something – the best, most satisfying meal you've ever eaten. Keira hates Cari, and I'm so, so glad.

'Yeah, she's cool,' I say.

'Hey, are we going to the mall?' says Keira loudly. 'Or standing around here all night? Come on!'

Grinning like mad, I follow James out into the night.

Chapter 8
She's the One

CARI.

'No! No, no! Ah . . .' A bolt of blue laserfire turns the screen black. Game over.

'Oh,' she says, letting go of the joystick and stepping away from the console. Raider Wars resets to challenge her to another round. I laugh at her expression.

'It takes practice,' I tell her over the steady thrum of pounding nonsense arcade music, the oddly modulated sounds of car engines and spaceships and gunfire. 'First time I played I lost by seven hundred points.'

'Whhhoooo!' yells Mikhal from across the aisle, where he's on a moveable cross bike. 'Take that, suckers!'

Cari crosses the aisle to take a closer look. 'Can you show me how to play that one?'

Swinging a leg over the seat, I put my foot to the pedal and rev the fake engine. She comes up behind and watches as I flog the guts out of the game, and when I reset it for her, she twists herself onto the seat in front of me with one fluid movement. She's sitting there, between my arms, her hands touching mine. The top of her head sits just below my chin. Her hair smells sweet from the shampoo, and soft strands of it tickle my nose. 'Here we go,' I say, hoping that she can't feel my heart thumping around in my chest. She leans too far into the first turn. I straighten up. 'Not so hard. Let the bike use the curve of the road . . . see? Watch it! There's a roadblock –'

She laughs as we smash wooden barriers into splinters.

'Turn the handle to throttle up – to go faster, right? We can take this jump pretty quick. Just make sure you keep...'

'Ah!'

'Crap!'

We're fried. A computer-generated body tumbles into the gorge, followed by a bike. She's shaking with laughter, leaning back a little now that she's let go of the handlebars. Her hair brushes against my cheek. I close my eyes for a moment. It's happening again, I can feel it, but not in a rush like the first time. It's slow, gentle, not painful. The smell of deodorant and body odour. The feel of movement, the hum of florescent lights, the taste of night-time . . . the colour of everything. It's all a thousand times brighter and it shines, everything, with its own pulsing glitter.

In slow motion, she turns her head against my shoulder. I don't ever want to move as she twists, looks up at me. Her lips move but I don't hear anything. Instead, I see her. Everything is too bright, I can't see much more than her standing there. But there must be others. I can hear them talking.

'... is this the only way?'

'Lena, be strong.'

'I will make sure . . .'

'Lena! No. We must do what is right.'

'I do not know that it is right.'

'Then you must trust, Lena. We must all trust.'

'I cannot. I cannot.' A long pause. 'Please, do this for me. Trust for me. I fear I am not strong enough . . .'

I'm standing there. Cari is standing there, watching all this, unseen. She turns a little and I see that horrible fear in her eyes. She's scared out of her mind.

She's running, now, across a narrow strip of a bridge. Wind pulls her hair back from her face, tripping her as it tangles her white smock around her legs. Slender strands, like golden spiders webs, net the sides of the bridge. She's moving too quickly. The bridge sways and jerks underneath her feet. She loses balance, falls against the strands, and they stretch – they stretch – and she pulls back, swaying, stumbling.

The figure that is chasing her is barely a vague form in the white mist. The narrow bridge quivers under their feet. There is no sound at all in this place; even the wind is silent. She leans into it, hard, but it pushes her back. She can barely put one foot in front of the other. She turns to see the figure pause also.

It is a woman. She's about Nina's height, with the same pale blonde hair and transparent skin that Cari has. She wears a long blue dress and her cheeks glisten with tears. Her lips move but make no sound.

The fear is visible in Cari's face; she knows what's coming. It's me that watches in surprised horror as the woman raises her arms and slashes the air with her hands. The silken filaments that hold the bridge tear under her fingernails. Like wires they snap, uncoiling, and the bridge drops and sways. Again, again she cuts. Cari tries to catch them in her hands, tries to hold them together, but it's useless. The bridge breaks apart around her. She screams as she falls . . .

And I'm holding her, holding her steady, holding myself steady against her. We don't say anything. Words have never seemed so useless.

But the world still exists. The flashing lights and formless noise of the arcade surrounds us. There's Mikhal whooping loudly because he beat the top score, and James yelling that he cheated. And there's Keira, hitting Baz over the head with one of the drumsticks from the virtual drumkit. Sucked back into the present, I feel changed. Nothing looks familiar. The night feels darker, the shadows deeper. Everyone is cheerful and oblivious. Keira looks up. The drumstick hangs loose in her hand as she sees me, and Cari. In the strobing neon light I can't tell what she's thinking, but she goes very, very still.

'I'm sick of this!' yells James, and the world clunks back into place. 'Who's up for pizza? Donnie's working at Pizza Place tonight.'

I take a deep breath, wondering if I'll be able to speak, but my voice is remarkably steady. 'We don't have to go,' I say in a low voice to Cari. 'There'll be meat there. Lots of it.'

But Cari smiles and takes my hand. 'We should go,' she says. 'I can tell you're having fun, and your friends will miss you if you leave.'

'Are you sure? I don't mind.' I really don't mind. I don't want to take her anywhere she doesn't want to be, and I'm selfishly thinking that I want to keep her all to myself right now. But she's already barging ahead to rejoin the group.

Pizza Place is full. Some little kid's having a birthday party, so the live entertainment consists of hyperactive seven-year-olds cramming ice-cream down each other's pants while their adult supervisors take turns ducking out for fresh air.

As we take a seat I notice Cari is stiffly trying not to wrinkle her nose, but she smiles at me and I promise myself I'll make this up to her.

Donnie gets us free pizza and Cokes while we bag him out for having to work on a Friday night. I reckon he spits in the pizza or something.

'Why don't you have some, Rebecca?' Keira asks around a mouthful of Cheese Supreme. 'It's good.'

'She's vegetarian,' I say, pushing the garlic bread in front of Cari. At least I know she'll enjoy that.

Mikhal pours his drink over Baz's pizza. Baz tries to stab him in the hand with a plastic fork. Keira tells them they can go over and join the kid's party if they're going to be so immature. Then she throws her pineapple pieces at them both.

Things are normal. Things are how they should be.

Until I go back to the dessert buffet for more jelly.

Suddenly Keira's beside me. 'So, Rebecca and you,' she says. She looks me straight in the eye. Downright, straightforward Keira – she speaks bluntly. 'You're going out?'

After what I just saw, what I experienced when she first touched me, after all this, I'm closer to Cari than anyone. My dad, my brother. None of them has ever let me inside their minds. I should be able to lie and say 'yes.' I should be able to brag about it, flaunt it in Keira's face. And yet, I shrug. 'I dunno.'

She nods. 'It's good,' she says. 'That's good.' And then, a smile. It's forced. She grasps my shoulder. 'See, Miles? It's exactly what you need, a woman to keep you in line!' And she's gone, back to the table, plonking herself down in Baz's lap.

I have a plate full of jelly, but no appetite at all.

***

Walking home, Cari says to me: 'She's the one, isn't she?'

'The one what? Who?'

'Keira. The one who makes you so purple-angry. When you were talking about school the other day, you looked like you did when you were around her tonight.'

'She doesn't make me angry. I just don't get why she's so stupid about things sometimes.'

'She likes him,' she presses on. 'He makes her laugh. She's happy when she's around him – I can see it, and you, who know her so well, can see it even more. That he helps her forget.'

'Forget what?'

'I don't know – I can't tell – whatever she needs to. People are like that, sometimes. They are drawn to those who distract them.'

'Keira doesn't need anyone to distract her. She's nuts, but she's the strongest person I've ever met. She doesn't care what people say. She doesn't let anyone push her around. She goes her own way. She doesn't need anyone.'

'Can you really know that?'

'Yes.' Keira is energy and movement. She's collected, contained. She's not like the rest of us – she knows exactly who she is and where she's going.

'Then why is she . . . how did you say it? Going out with him?'

I'm struck by the question. We've stopped walking and Cari is looking at me questioningly. Our breath is solid in the air between us, a wall of drifting cloud. I struggle for an answer. Because she wants to make me jealous? Because she's in love with him? Because she's bored, or confused, or . . . none of those reasons make any sense either. They're not Keira.

Can you really know that?

'Oh!'

It's a small gasp, barely audible. Cari is holding out her hand, and there on her sleeve is a tiny white flake. A heartbeat later and another joins it. In unison we both turn our eyes skywards. Soft white flakes are filling the air, swirling in the stillness. The entire world seems to go silent.

'What is it?' Cari breathes.

'Snow,' I say. 'It's snow. We've never had it here before, at least, not while I've been alive.'

'It's beautiful.'

'Yeah,' I agree. 'It's really beautiful.'

Chapter 9
White World

NINA is still up when we get home. She gives me the third degree for not calling her to pick us up. 'You know what happens to kids who walk around the streets at night?' she says shrilly. 'You won't just get mugged, you'll get murdered. Rebecca, I'm taking you home.'

'Can't she stay over? It's snowing, you know.'

'No.' She's already got her car keys. 'You can't just do whatever you feel like . . .'

She pauses, having just caught a glimpse through the window. The snow is piling up on the window-ledge. The world outside is white. 'We'll wait till it stops.'

'It's piling up pretty thick,' I tell her. 'It probably won't melt until morning.'

I'm surprised, but Nina is just as mesmerised as we were by the snow. Maybe it has that calming effect on everyone. 'You know, I don't think I've ever seen snow as thick as this,' she says. 'I'll have to call your parents, Rebecca.'

'She already did. Sent them a text message, I mean. They were going to pick her up but the snow is coming down even thicker on the other side of town. If she could just stay over, they wouldn't have to worry.'

Nina sighed. 'Well, I guess it won't hurt. I'll lend her some pyjamas and set up the couch. Go and sit in front of the heater and warm up, hey? Make yourselves some Milo.'

***

Daniel wakes up when I shut the door. He blinks sleepily, then sits up. 'Wow!' He sticks to the window like one of those stupid suction animals people put in their cars. But I'm in too much of a good mood to kick him off my bed. 'That's so cool. Hey, do you reckon we can go out and build a snowman?'

'Yeah, only if you want Nina to bury you in the snow beside it.'

'Will it still be there in the morning? Maybe if it stays till Monday we won't have to go to school. Like in the movies!'

'Maybe.' I pull the blankets up.

'Jake?' he says thoughtfully. 'Can I tell you something?'

I nod, even though he can't see it in the darkness.

'I think Dad's having an affair.'

'What? What makes you think that? Do you even know what an affair is?'

'I know what it is,' he says. 'I heard Nina say

it. On the phone before. She was talking to one of her friends.'

'No, no. I'm pretty sure you heard wrong.'

'I know what I heard. That's what she said. I'm not lying.'

'I know you're not lying! But geez, Dan, that's a big call to make. I just don't see why she would say that.' My heart is thumping loudly. 'Do you think he's having an affair?'

'He never comes home,' he says solemnly. 'And when he does, he yells at Nina. Maybe he hates her.'

'Dad does not hate Nina. Even if he was having an affair . . .' What am I saying? 'No, Dan, I mean . . .' I don't know what I mean. Daniel's completely right. I've hardly seen Dad in about three weeks. Geez, maybe he is having an affair! I wouldn't know. 'I don't think we should jump to conclusions. There could be a thousand reasons why. Whatever you heard Nina say, she was just guessing. It doesn't mean anything.'

'What if he decides to leave?'

I stare at his wide-eyed face. He's scared, the poor kid. I'm so mad at both of them right now. Can't they see what they're doing to him? It's not fair. He's too young to be worrying about anything except when they move his favourite cartoon to a different time-slot.

'Daniel,' I say very calmly. 'Dad is not going to leave. Not without us.'

He turns away from me. I don't think I was

very convincing. I certainly didn't convince myself.

'They sky looks so weird,' he says. 'Up there. It's almost like the clouds are hard. You could touch them. And the way they're all piled up like that . . ..'

'In the morning,' I promise. 'We'll build a snowman.'

Chapter 10
Mrs Henders

I'M right. The snow lasts until morning, and starts up again in little flurries even as it gets lighter. I finally pull myself out of bed, and discover that the Daniel's bed is empty.

He's in the lounge room, talking to Cari. The little bugger is talking to Cari.

Crap.

'... when you fire it. Like that.'

A slap and a clunk, and Daniel's giggle. I look through the door. He's curled up on the couch in Cari's doona, and she's sitting cross-legged beside him, holding his slingshot loosely in one hand, and a rubber ball in the other. A similar ball is now bouncing between the TV cabinet and the wall.

'I don't think you want to be doing that in-side,' I say.

'Oh! Good morning,' says Cari. She's smiling warmly. 'Daniel is showing me slingshots. I've seen these in books, but now I know how they work.'

'Nina's gone out for milk. She had to walk.

The driveway is so covered in snow she can't get the car out.' Daniel says this like it's the best thing in the world.

'What about Dad?'

'I dunno.' And this, like he couldn't care less. I'm a bit shocked by it. 'Nina's going to make pancakes, though.'

I try to ignore it, but the magic of the snow pulls at me until I'm standing outside, running my hands through the soft, powdery stuff. Cold trickles of it run down my arms. I shiver in delight.

Daniel bounds out the door behind me. 'Snowfight!'

The neighbourhood kids have gone nuts. They're tearing up and down the carless road, skidding and sliding, hurling snow at anything and everything, and screaming their heads off while they're at it. And it's not just the kids that are out. Men and women are walking around, just looking at the change wrought on familiar places by this strange phenomenon. Down the road, an old man is trying to shovel the snow off his car using a rubber scuba-flipper and swearing heavily about being late for work. The old couple who live a few doors away are sitting on their brick fence with steaming mugs of coffee. It's like another world.

Cari comes up behind me. She's looking wary. 'That woman,' she whispers. I turn a little. Sure enough, number forty-seven is standing on her veranda, watching.

'Don't worry about her,' I whisper.

***

We build a snowman. Well, a snow-thing. It's not as easy as in the movies, and the snow is too fresh, not hard-packed like it should be. When we roll the torso into place the whole things starts to droop to one side, but I don't think any of us cares. Our fingers are frozen and we're having fun.

'Looks like he's drunk,' says a voice from behind us

It takes me a while to recognise Keira under all the layers of scarves and coats and beanies. And besides, she doesn't have Baz attached to her elbow. She pokes Snowman in the gut. 'Beer belly.'

'Like to see you do any better,' I mutter.

'Hi Keira!' sings Daniel, before he slams a ball of snow into her face.

'Uh.' Wiping it off, she smiles at Cari. 'Hi, Rebecca. I'm glad you came out last night. Good movie, hey?'

'Yeah,' Cari replies.

'We'll do it again. I just came round because we need to talk about our project, Jake.' Jake. Jake. Since when has she ever called me Jake? 'I've had an idea. It's perfect.'

'Yeah?'

She spreads her arms. 'I just thought of it this morning. It's been staring us in the face.'

My good humour is gone, wiped out under a wash of irritation. 'What?'

'Look around! It's a science experiment in itself.'

'Snow? I think we all know how snow is formed, Keira. It's hardly . . .'

'God. Do I have to spell it out for you then?' her voice is sharp. 'The weather. Global warming. Climate change. What we're doing to ourselves by pumping out carbon gasses. How much worse it's going to get . . . you know? We could do a model. Predict the next decade. It's gold.'

It's a good idea. She's right, it'll probably get us a good grade if we do it right. A model . . . we could look at the wind patterns, temperature rises, all that – chart them over the last five years, graph them for the next ten . . .

'Geez, you'd never think it would be so hard to find a bottle of milk. The way people are acting you'd think the world's coming to an end. One stupid woman ahead of me got fifteen bottles . Fifteen! I had to fight just to get one, and it cost me two dollars twenty... oh, hello Keira. Do you want some pancakes?' Nina slams through the door and vanishes. Rubbing the feeling back into our hands, we traipse after her.

Chapter 11
Ice Storm

'SO what, we need to look up the Bureau of Meteorology? Maybe we could talk to Mike Mathers, you know, Channel Seven News.'

Daniel and Cari are in the lounge room, where Daniel is introducing our guest to the wonderful world of Japanese animation. Keira and I sit at the table, a pile of pancakes and a notebook between us.

Keira rolls her eyes. 'Yeah, and that's about as interesting as my left elbow.. Nah, this is what we're going to do, right? Basically, we want to know the correlation between global warming and our wonderful little winter wonderland out there. But we're going to call it 'The Next Ice Age: the Dawn of a New Civilisation.' Okay. So how does this new world work?'

I stare at her. Everyone's staring at her. Does she expect me to answer? 'Um . . .'

'Cars don't work in sub-zero temperatures. And being outside without proper protective clothing, well, you can forget that. Entire forests would be wiped out. And what about crops?'

'Hydroponic bays,' I say slowly.

'So a small group of people gets a monopoly on the food supply. What happens then? Price-hikes, right?'

'The underprivileged can't afford food,' I say. 'And what about third-world countries?'

Keira slaps a hand on the table. 'Hah!'

'Nina, maybe we could talk to your friend. The one who works at the EPA? About what might happen to animals . . .'

'What? Oh, yes. Yeah.' She's poking at the remaining pancake mix. I don't think she even heard me.

It's the simplest of ideas but it really is a good one. If we do it the right way we can get top marks without a hitch. Mr Jass will love it. And me, I'm breathing in Keira's enthusiasm. Watching her come alive like this is intoxicating. 'I'll write down some stuff. We'll do some more tomorrow, okay? Baz and I were going to go down to the skate park but maybe we could all hang out or something.'

'Maybe,' I say, losing my eagerness.

'I'll ask him tonight on my way home. My phone's dead so I can't call him, but his house isn't too far away. I'll see you tomorrow, okay?'

When she leaves, bundled in extra jackets and scarves, it almost hurts.

'It's started snowing again!' says Daniel. He's bouncing in the doorway.

I hadn't even noticed, but now I hear the rising howl of the wind. Something is banging around on the garage roof. Nina lifts the blinds, and through the tangled branches of the bushes I see that the world has turned from white to grey. The clouds are low and menacing, and snow is coming down in thick flurries. There must be ice in with it to make it fall so fast. It pastes the window and clings to the trees.

'Go and tell Rebecca to call her dad,' Nina tells Daniel. 'She'll have to stay here until it all clears. I hope your other friend will be all right, walking home in this.'

The window rattles with the wind. I'm alone with Nina and the silence rings loudly in my ears.

She's just standing there. At the sink, with the empty bowl in her hands. She's staring through the window at the storm beyond.

It bursts out of my mouth. 'It's just the weather, right? Dad, I mean. He's stuck at work.'

'He's staying in a hotel,' she replies, too quickly, and begins to scrub the bowl. Far too hard. 'Can't possibly drive.'

'No,' I say. 'He'll be back tomorrow, though.'

'Once the roads are clear. Of course.'

'Nina,' I say, hesitate, and then it bursts out. 'Do you think he's cheating on you?'

'No.' The answer is too sharp, too fast. Even she realises this, and when she turns to face me she can't hide the uncertainty in her eyes.

She sighs, drops her tea towel and seems to collapse into a chair at the table. 'I don't know.

He won't talk to me. He's so tired all the time, so quiet, and he won't say anything about his work, or the extra pressure he's been under. And all this extra time he's spending away . . . it just makes me wonder, that's all. It's unfair, I know. He's never given me cause to think these things. But that doesn't stop them from cropping up in your thoughts, you know?'

I nod. I know.

'I don't think he's cheating on you either.' It's all I can say. She looks up with this tired little smile, and I think that for once I might have said the right thing.

***

I find Cari in the lounge room with Daniel. She's obviously graduated from Neon Genesis Evangelion — now she's holding an XBOX controller and staring at the TV. The crackle of gunfire and Daniel saying, 'No, you've killed a civilian! You'll have to start again.'

I glance through the window, but it's fogged over with condensation. It's pretty cold in here, too, even with the heater on. I head upstairs to take a shower, but the thin trickle of water that comes out is freezing cold. The cold is really taking its toll on the poor water heater. I grab my jacket and head outside to check the temperature gauge.

It's hard to force the door open against the

wind. The cold seeps through everything I'm wearing in an instant, and the air is like solid ice in my lungs. I pull my jacket tight and wade through the snow to the side of the house. Our snowmen have vanished under the fresh fall, and the road is barely visible. A car comes around the corner. Its headlights are on high beam and it's crawling, windscreen wipers waving frantically, and it almost happens in slow motion; a small jerk, a shriek of tyres, the car slewing to one side. The driver panics – brake lights glowing angry red and the car snakes across the road, coming to a stop by the kerb, sideways across the road.

I stop at the corner of the porch. She's there, number forty-seven, and staring straight at me.

I smile shakily.

She's wearing a tartan skirt and red cardigan, so that she looks like a bloodstain against the whiteness. Her pink flamingo ornaments are heaped over with snow, making irregular little mounds all over her lawn.

'Do you know?' she says. Her voice carries across the space easily. 'Can you see it yet?'

'See what?' I say. 'The . . . the . . .'

'The city. The city in the sky. Can you see what she is?'

There is no point in pretending. 'I have seen bits of it. Pieces. I don't know what she is. I don't think I can.'

She nods approvingly. 'Nor will you ever. Which is why it's best.'

'What's best?'

'She can't stay here. See the damage this has caused already.' She sweeps her hands wide. 'Imagine what will happen if it's not fixed.'

'What?' I'm angry now. 'Why can't you just say what you mean? I'm sick of this! Stop speaking in riddles and say something useful! What do you mean, the damage this has caused? The snow isn't Cari's fault. It started before . . . before she fell!' I protest. 'She wasn't even here when the frosts started. That was weeks ago.'

'Ah.' The old woman almost, almost smiles. 'But she was there. It was there. The city of ice and silver light. '

I remember what Cari said. It's always been there. Shar. The first city, and the last. I remember what I saw when I touched her at the arcade. That woman slashing the bridge, causing Cari to fall . . .

The city of ice and silver light.

What if – what if when Cari fell, when that bridge was cut from under her, she broke through something, and bought part of her world with her? But it doesn't make sense. The ice did start weeks ago. She couldn't have brought it with her. I call out – 'hey' – but Mrs Henders is already shuffling away.

I forget about the water heater. I'll have a shower in the morning.

Chapter 12
The Telescope

NIGHT seems to fall faster than it should. We watch reports of car crashes, hypothermia cases, and missing persons on the TV. There's no word from Dad, and before we go to bed, the storm rises again. Daniel is ecstatic.

I'm still awake at midnight. It's freezing cold as I slip out of bed and pull on my dressing gown. The moon shines clear on the fallen snow, casting thick bands of solid silver light through the frost-covered windows.

Cari is awake, of course. She's sitting on the couch, her blankets drawn up to her chin.

I sit down beside her.

'Your world is changing,' she whispers.

I'm thinking of what Mrs Henders said. 'I've never seen anything like this. No one ever has. Australia is a dry country, and this . . . this is insane.'

She stands up then, letting the blankets fall away. She moves to stand in a patch of the moonlight. It streams through her hair. She raises her arms and turns a slow circle, as if to soak it into her skin.

'My world basks in silver light.'

I close my eyes, hardly able to bear looking at her. 'I need to know. You know what I mean, Cari. Whatever happened – it has ruined the boundary between your world and mine. Look out there! The snow, the ice, the silver light – they're of your world, not mine. This is not about you. It's about everyone. In both our worlds.'

She drops her arms, kneels on the floor. She does not meet my eyes.

'Cari.' Something cold is clawing in my stomach. 'I'm not going to be mad.'

She does not move.

'Mrs Henders – the lady next door, she seems to know things. She said . . . she seems to think your arrival somehow made this happen. I don't see how that's possible. The ice started weeks ago, before you arrived. But she says if whatever is wrong isn't fixed . . . well, I need to know if it can be fixed. My world can't go on like this.'

Her eyes, slowly, rise to meet mine. And there is that horrible fear, that look as if she's poised to run. I feel the tension of her body. I'm careful not to move.

'Do you look up at the stars, Jake?'

I smile. 'A lot, yeah.'

'Why?'

It's another of her odd questions. 'Because .. . I don't know. I think they're comforting.' I shake my head. 'No, that's not true. There's nothing comforting about them. They've been the way they are for thousands of years, but we still don't really understand a lot about how they got there, or why they are the way they are.'

'I know this feeling. But in the city, in Shar, when I look out, I can see the lights of your world. They're so bright, and there are so many of them. They share our sky, and yet we have so little understanding of them. Of how they got there, or why they are the way they are.'

'So people in your world don't know that we exist? Just as we have no idea about Shar?'

She nods. 'They have some little understanding. As I said, there are those who have crossed over. They are carefully guarded, and not allowed to speak to anyone. Those who speak with them are sworn to secrecy. It is for our own good, they say. Should the knowledge fall into the wrong hands . . .'

'What do you mean? What would happen? What could possibly be so bad?'

'You don't know?' she says. 'Oh, but of course. There are men and women who keep secrets in your world as well.'

'Secrets about what? Cari, stop being so cryptic!'

'About your world and how it is dying,' she replies.

'It's not dying.' I stare at her in astonishment. 'It's not! It's been here for hundreds of years. It can't die.'

'But it is. The clouds are gathering. Thick poisonous smoke stretches across the lights. They're not as bright as they used to be. And we can see the storms, and the lack of them. We can see the dryness and the flooding. And we can see you driving cars and cutting trees and burning coal to try and make more lights, as if somehow you can keep from noticing the dark spaces if only it's bright enough . . .'

'Your people think . . .' I gabble, stupidly. 'They think that if we knew about your world, we'd invade?'

'Once your own is gone, yes.'

'But that's stupid! That's the stupidest thing I ever heard!'

'Would it be stupid to try and survive?'

Her measured look brooks no argument, because it is true. If some people on Earth found out about Shar, it wouldn't last an hour.

'I was so curious about your kind. I watched the people of your world. I learned about your schools and your food and things like Daniel's slingshots. I was fascinated, but it wasn't enough. So I stole a forbidden book. I read it, and I needed to know more. And it only made me want to know more. Greedily I hunted for papers, manuscripts, anything with reference to your world. It consumed me. I suppose . . . no, I didn't ever think that no one would notice. I just thought my own curiosity was justification enough, and I grew careless.'

'And someone found out that you were looking into things you weren't supposed to. That's why that woman cut the bridge.'

She shakes her head now. 'No. If it were only that I'd disobeyed them, I think I would have been scolded, disgraced, but not . . . not cast out.'

'Then what did you do? Cari, you have to tell me.'

She yells, 'No I don't! I don't have to tell anyone anything!'

'This is important!'

'LEAVE ME ALONE!' She shouts this with such vehemence that I'm shocked. Her face is twisted in anger. She looks so different, I'm almost afraid of her. I can't say anything else. I stand up and walk back to my room.

***

Daniel is perched on my bed. He's pressed up against the window, but it takes me a while to realise what he's doing.

'What's that?'

But I know what he's got in his hands. He turns slowly, lowering the telescope and looking at me in dumbstruck awe.

'Bloody hell.' My voice doesn't sound like it's my own. 'Why can't you just leave things alone?'

'Because you never tell me anything!' he returns, his voice shrill. 'You never tell me!

There's a . . . in the sky . . . it's a city – a frigging city, Jake!'

'There's nothing –'

'NO!' he yells. 'Don't do that! You always do it, but I'm not stupid! Don't act like I don't know what's really going on!'

'You don't know what's going on! Give me that.'

'I know there's something weird about Rebecca. The way she talks, and acts, and knows about some things and nothing about other stuff – stuff that everyone knows. And with you sneaking around at night and talking to number forty-seven, I'd know something was going on even if I was as stupid as you think I am.'

'Whatever you reckon you know, it doesn't give you the right to pinch my stuff. '

'Where did you get it from, anyway?'

I take a deep breath. 'Mrs Henders gave it to me.'

'Why? Why would she give it to you? Come on, Jake, I'm your brother. Why don't you trust me?'

'Keep your voice down. I couldn't tell anyone. Not just you – I couldn't tell Dad, or Nina – anyone. No one can know about what's up there.'

'Why not?'

I struggle to find an answer. Daniel sees only my hesitation.

'It's always like this. You don't think I'll understand so you don't tell me, because somehow that makes it better for me. Like Nina and Dad, when you say everything's all right and you know it's not. I hate it! I hate you!'

'Dan! Shut up before you wake Nina.'

And he does. He drops the telescope on my bed and clambers over to his. He pulls the covers up over his head and turns away from me.

I sit on the edge of my bed. 'That's it, you know,' I say after a while to his unmoving back. 'I can't exactly come up to you and say, "There's a city in the sky". I kind of thought I was going nuts. I'm glad you've seen it too.'

'It's really beautiful.' His muffled voice comes from under his pillow.

'Yeah.' I take a deep breath. 'Dan, Rebecca isn't her real name. I just called her that because she wouldn't tell me what her name was. See, it happens to me too.' I laugh. 'I think everyone finds it hard to trust when they don't know how other people are going to react.'

There's a pause. 'She looks like she comes from there.'

There, I suppose, means the city. 'Yeah, she does, doesn't she. She's made of the same kind of stuff.'

'Then why is she here?'

'I don't know exactly. Something happened, something changed. After Mrs Henders gave me the telescope, she told me she reckons Cari did something, and Cari says she was exiled, thrown out. And now she can't go back.'

'But she has to!'

He sits up, throwing off his covers and staring at me earnestly. 'She can't stay here. Where's she going to live? Whatever she did, it can't have been bad. She can't have murdered anyone or anything. She can't stay here – this isn't her home.'

'I know.' I sigh. 'And she knows it too. But I don't know how to fix it.'

'Nina could help us. If we got her to look through the telescope, she'd have to believe us!'

I shake my head. 'Honestly, Dan, I don't think she would.' I don't think Nina's mind is made that way. If we showed her, she'd think it was a lovely trick and ask us how we're doing it. I think about Dad, and realise he wouldn't even look through the telescope in the first place – "I don't have time right now, but show me later".

'I know.' His shoulders slump. 'But you said Mrs Henders knows something. And if she gave you the telescope . . . '

It hits me then, that wave of brilliance, and I reach over to thump Daniel's shoulder. 'You're amazing sometimes!'

'I'm coming with you, you know.' he says warningly.

I know steel restraints wouldn't keep him from following me back to the lounge room. Cari is standing there, having been woken by the soft noises we make coming down the hall. She looks at me balefully, and though I want to say something, I can't find the words. Daniel's smile has turned shy now that he knows the truth, and he edges past her as if she might hit him.

But she follows us outside. Wearing only the pyjamas Nina leant her, she walks bare-foot through the snow drifts. Daniel and I struggle against the wind, slipping and skidding on the ice. The wind has not relented. It slaps our faces and stings alarmingly.

'Look,' Daniel hisses.

She is already there, waiting for us. Like Cari, she stands atop the snow, wearing no protection from the cold.

'It took you a while,' she says.

Chapter 13
Mrs Henders' Story

WHENEVER a stray ball has sailed over the fence into Mrs Henders' yard, it has been abandoned. We'd watch it grow flat and slowly decay for months before it vanished into the earth – neither of us ever daring to venture past the gate to fetch it or to ask for its return. Now, as we follow the old woman up the path, I think we all feel a sense of displacement. Of being where we're not supposed to be.

Mrs Henders walks swiftly. She stands impatient at the door, and huffs a breath when we take so long to cross the threshold. 'Don't bother,' she snaps as we try to stamp the snow off our shoes, but it feels wrong as we tread icy muck into the carpet. I can smell old wallpaper and burnt matches.

There is one light on in the house, in the kitchen, and it's towards this that we head. The house is old, set out with steps and wooden floors. The kitchen is done in yellow linoleum, cracked and peeling, and an ancient iron stove sits in the corner. It gives out the most delicious heat. The room is shabby and close, with jam jars and books, bottles and little porcelain ornaments and other odds and ends piled onto spare surfaces. There are at least a hundred framed photos hanging on the walls. I feel surprisingly comfortable.

She motions that we should sit at the table. Daniel drags his chair closer to the fire.

'The dark-haired woman know you're here?'

'Nina doesn't know,' I tell her.

'So, get on with it. It's late.'

I hold out the telescope. 'Why did you give me this?'

'Why do you think?'

'So I could see the city? But why did you want me to? Why did you think I needed to?'

'Because you did need to.'

'Well, why? To help Cari? I can't help her anyway! So what good does it do?'

'I don't know,' she says.

'But you know things!' blurts out Daniel. 'You knew about Cari.'

'You knew that she fell,' I chime in. 'And you knew that I knew. And . . . I think I know how, and why.' I look at her now, at her hard, cold eyes, her tightly-bound hair, her softened, sagging skin.

'It was a long time ago,' she says, her eyes firmly fixed on Cari. 'I thought it was part of a different life, one I'd never have to face again. Then, a few weeks ago, I felt the chill in the air. Not just the normal chill of winter on this world,

but a deeper, icier coldness. I took out my telescope and I looked into the sky. And I saw your
thread piercing the veil between our worlds.'

'The golden strand,' I say. 'Cari, you made
that?'

'What is it?' Daniel asks.

But Cari doesn't answer. She's gazing at Mrs
Henders in awe. 'You are from Shar as well.'

'I was, once. Now it seems like I am more
from this world than that one. Oh, I kept the
telescope. I clung to it, my last remaining link,
like a lifeline. Such a thing should not exist in
this world. If it fell into the wrong hands, it
could mean disaster for us all. But after all my
work, after all it had cost me, I hadn't the heart
to destroy it.'

'I'm so sorry,' I whisper. 'I had no idea.'

She waves a hand. 'A long time ago.'

'You can't have forgotten your home.'

'Of course not. Memory is a cruel thing, and
you can't choose what fades and what stays fast.
Still I long to return, every hour, every minute.
But it is a dulled pain, a pain of habit, a guilty
indulgence. Perhaps I should say, rather, that I
have given it up. Like a habit, I have quit.' A dry
chuckle escapes her unsmiling lips.

'You don't want to return?'

'What I want doesn't matter.'

'But surely if you could . . .'

'You aren't listening,' she hisses. 'I cannot
return. I waited too long. And now I don't
belong there any more than I do here.'

'But that –' Cari is adamant, pleading. Her face is creased with concern and fear. 'That –'

'You think you can do these things without consequence? Mess with the fabric of worlds and expect no recourse? It is not so. When I made this –' she points to the telescope, 'this thing, I intended to study the people of this world. In Shar I was a scientist. Or what you would call a scientist in this world – I studied movements and energies, particularly those surrounding the bridges between our worlds. I was trying to find out how to keep the bridges stable and anchored. In the course of my research I discovered that using glass treated with heat and glazes would filter the lights and strip the veil between our worlds, giving me a clear view directly into the forests, the hospitals, the schools, even people's lounge rooms if I chose to look that closely. I thought I had made a brilliant discovery.

'Instead, my invention tore through the boundaries. Just by looking, I was poking holes in the delicate fabric that keeps our worlds separate.

'Just like you, girl. You pierced the veil with your golden thread.'

'I only wanted to learn,' Cari said. 'I wanted to see things more closely.'

'Just like you, I thought the rules were mere impositions, created by us, and able to be broken. You must understand this thing that is hardest of all to comprehend for us mortals –

that we are not gods. In the universe, we are nothing. When I crossed over, I bought a blast of coldness with me. Thankfully I knew enough to seal the boundary behind me, so that the ice did not take over. As it has now.'

Cari is crying. Silent tears roll over her cheeks.

'I have to go home,' Cari whispers.

'I sacrificed my right to belong to either world the moment I conceived the thought of crossing the boundary. Even when I was stranded here, exiled, and clinging to the idea of finding a way back, I think I knew that I would never walk in my world again. Even if I found a way back, they would not let me live there. They'd cast me back, or imprison me, just as they have done with the countless others who have crossed over.'

'It's not the same for me,' Cari begs. 'It's not! I can go home! They will forgive me. They will. I will never speak a word of what I've seen and done in this world. I will never think of it again.'

'You show your youth, thinking that will be enough,' says Mrs Henders. 'Even if you could somehow manage to find a way to return. You have spent too long in this world already. It's changed you.'

'It hasn't,' protests Cari. 'Not that much. I've only been here a few days.'

'The longer you stay, the more it will affect you. Just as it did me. Do you think my name was 'Mrs Addie Henders' when I lived in Shar?'

She points to the wall, at the framed photos hanging there. I look at them closely for the first time. They are photos of her – Mrs Henders – as a younger girl, with long pale hair and striking eyes. She is smiling as she poses on a beach, holding a fishing rod, struggling to hold onto a kite. There are group photos with friends, and others where she has her arm around a man with dark hair – her husband? It's clear that she's lived almost a lifetime while she's been here.

'I got a job. A house. A name. I married a man and for a while I loved him. And he loved the person he thought was me – it's not like I could ever tell him the truth. I spent all this time hiding and pretending to be someone else. That is my punishment.'

Her lips curl up in a sneer.

'It'll happen to you too. You'll realise it's too late to go back. You're tainted. You have breathed it in, the fumes, the stench, the fear and hate, the waste and hunger, the ruined dreams and monstrous greed.'

'– And the fear of shadows, the brightness of lights to block out the darkness, to block out the stars, the warmth, movies and Milo, and computer games and the utter strangeness of everything! Of people who love so deeply they can't see it, of people torn up inside because they don't want to admit what they want, or what they need. Do we not have those things in our world? Do we exist above hate and hunger?

Did I not long to know what lay on the other side of the bridges? Did I not despise the woman who stranded me here?'

Cari is breathing hard, her eyes blazing with anger. 'We were wrong. In refusing to acknowledge this world, we have thought ourselves superior and ignored the fact that we are so similar. That we are linked so closely. And whether these things are bad, whether they are good, whether they've changed me or whether they were always there in my life, I'll take it all back with me. I take it all.'

She turns and is gone. The front door bangs closed. Daniel and I are left staring at Mrs Henders.

Somehow her hair has worked its way loose, and a curl of silver falls over her forehead. She suddenly doesn't look so hunched, so glowering, or so strange. She looks exactly like an old woman.

'Do you want to go back?'

It's Daniel's question. He looks worried. It's too grave a look for someone so young.

But the look fades as Mrs Henders does something unexpected – she smiles. 'I'd never be able to own pink flamingo garden ornaments in that world.'

Chapter 14
Morning

CARI says nothing when we creep back into the house at last that night. She curls up on the couch. My heart aches for her. To be told you must give up your home, that you could never go back, is beyond anything I can imagine. What can I possibly say to her? Nothing would make it any better, any easier to bear. So I climb into bed and stare at the wall. Sleep, when it does come, is a panicked rush of fear. I wake up with the certain knowledge that something is really wrong.

The phone shouldn't be ringing this early.

The worried voice on the other end of the line has my heart plunging into an abyss. At first I think it must be about Dad. Car crash, I think. Falling tree. Building collapsed . . . The ringing in my ears makes it hard to hear.

'. . . not answering her mobile phone. I know she was at your house yesterday evening, working on the science project, because I asked her for your parents' phone number before she left.'

'Oh,' I say, relieved to realise that it's Mrs Leichman, Keira's mum. 'Keira went to Baz's last night, after we finished studying. To ask him about something. Her phone battery died and she was going to ask him about his plans for today, I think.'

'Baz? You mean Barry, the boy she's been hanging around with? Are you sure that's where she went?'

And suddenly I'm not sure about anything. I suddenly grasp what Mrs Leichman is saying. Keira never made it home. That panicked feeling is back, but it's increased tenfold. 'Yeah, of course. She left here last night,' I say, as new fears twine together. 'Early. Just before . . . ' oh shit, ' . . . the storm hit. She went to Baz's.. Um, I've got his dad's home number.' I read it out to her.

'I'm just worried,' she says, trying to sound calm. 'There have been so many accidents. I'd like to know where she is.'

'Me too,' I tell her, earnestly.

I'm fighting to keep my heart in my chest as I dial Baz's mobile number.

'Piss OFF,' he moans the second he picks up. I can tell he's just rolled over in bed.

'Did she get to your place last night?' I ask urgently. 'Keira.'

'No, man. I mean, was she supposed to? Why?'

'Oh no,' I murmur.

'Miles . . . '

'She left before the storm hit last night.'

'What? Why didn't you call me?' He's angry. What can I say? I had more important things to think about at the time? It's the truth – the selfish, ugly truth.

'Her mum is calling your dad now. We should try a couple of her friends' places,' I say desperately.

If she was walking to Baz's house she would have taken the Garter Street bridge, and Sally's place is just on the other side. But no one answers the phone, and when I send Sally a text I get an answer from the network that service is unavailable. I try Keira's mobile phone myself, just in case, but just like her mum said, there is no answer. 'Jake.'

It's Daniel, and I can tell by his face that he's heard everything.

'Is it Keira? Is she lost?'

'No one's seen her,' I tell him. 'She's not answering her phone, and no one knows where she was last night. Her mum's probably called the police.'

'But there's hundreds of people missing,' he says.

I nod. I've already thought of that.

Cari is in the doorway. Her pale skin is almost translucent.

Daniel and I look at one another. 'I'll grab the coats,' I say. 'We have to go before Nina comes down.'

***

Outside it's a nightmare. There are odd formations everywhere; my mind struggles to equate this uncanny landscape with the familiar street on which I've lived my entire life. It just doesn't seem to fit.

The wind is so cold. I think Daniel feels it most of all; he kind of hunches over, as if by not moving he'll keep from getting any colder, but he doesn't utter a word of complaint. Cari's hair is whipped back from her face, and she breathes deeply the frozen air. She's in her native element here.

'Her house is on Highland Street,' I say. 'She probably did go towards the bridge. Um . . . she would have gone through the park, cutting across the path by the lakes.'

'Unless she took the shortcut,' said Daniel. 'You know?'

'What, you mean through the plantation?' I look at the dark green trees across the frozen tundra of the Phoenix Park. It looks even darker in there than usual. 'She knows the way just as well as we do, but it would have been too dark.'

'Would that stop her?'

I laugh. No, nothing would stop Keira.

Once the dark limbs have closed overhead, I know there was no way I would have gone on had I been alone in the dark. The snow provides an extra layer of insulation, and it is completely silent within. The trees seem taller, closer. The pine needles crackle and slide underfoot.

We know the plantation pretty well, Daniel and I. We've spent hours and hours here hiding from Mum and Dad – but it was a huge place and we'd never been through the whole area. There were countless crags and gullies hidden by gorse and shadow. I keep a close eye on Cari, to make sure she doesn't slip or fall. It's not necessary. She seems to know exactly where to step, and doesn't slip once.

None of us says what we're thinking. If she did come this way, the only reason she wouldn't have made it home was if she was hurt or lost. And if either of those things were true, how could we possibly find her?

'Keira!' Daniel calls, but he only does it once. The resounding echo is too loud, too unsettling.

The idea of actually finding her seems so hopeless, now. In my mind she is sprawled on the ground, unconscious and bloody, at the bottom of a ravine. Snow has already buried her.

'Do people die in your world?' Daniel asks.

I stop still. Cari turns towards Daniel, her eyes wide. I think if I touched her now, the flood of emotions would kill me.

'Yes,' she says. 'We have that in common. But the ice . . . no one dies in the ice.'

'How come?'

'I cannot explain it. I don't know how.' She looks around her. 'In our world the ice is part of things. Just like air.'

'Keira's not dead,' I snap. I'm angry. Them talking about death makes the possibility of it real. 'I think we need to head towards the bridge. We can double back if we don't find her there and go through this whole area.'

Even as I say it, it rings in my ears as a vast, vast impossibility.

My phone rings. I stare at the screen. 'It's Nina.'

'Don't answer,' says Daniel.

I flick it onto silent mode.

'She's going to be worried,' Daniel cautioned.

'Of course she is.' I tap out a quick text – we're fine – and shove it back in my pocket. I feel incredibly guilty about doing it, but I couldn't give into it. 'You want to go back?'

'No,' Daniel says. 'You know she's worried because she cares about us.'

I kick at a tree stump. 'Why? I don't get it. She's not part of our family. She just walks in one night with Dad and never leaves. Like we're her family. Like she's . . .'

'Mum.'

'She's not,' I say sharply. 'She can't pretend she is.'

'I don't think she is.'

'Why are you sticking up for her?'

'Because she's still there.'

We're standing in a circle now, our breath forming a solid cloud between us, cold faces barely visible under our caps. I look from Daniel to Cari and back. 'What?'

'Mum's not. And Dad's not,' Daniel says. 'But she is.'

I'm speechless. How can he say that? How can he betray Mum like that? And Dad? For Nina? She's . . . she's . . . I want to say that we don't need her to be there. Daniel and I are fine on our own. But it sounds like a spoiled child sulking about having been told off. Because what he says is true – Nina doesn't owe us anything. But she's stuck around for two years.

'I reckon if I climbed up there, I could see.' Daniel's voice breaks into my thoughts. I hadn't even realised it, but we were standing below our old treehouse, and he's pointing up to it. It is a jumble of rotten wood wedged in the branches now, half-covered in white snow. I remember building it, and how we could see the entire area from up there.

'No way. There's ice and snow everywhere. You could slip.'

'I could slip on the ground, too,' he protests, then sighs. 'Fine. I'm taking a toilet break.'

'Don't go too far.'

He gives me a withering glance, as if to say there's a girl present, then vanishes into the misty darkness.

'Sometimes I reckon he's actually more mature than I am,' I say.

Cari looks amused. 'I think we could learn much from the honesty of children.'

'Is that what it is? The way he sees things that I just can't? It freaks me out.'

'He has not forgotten your mother, Jake. He never will.'

I feel tears sting my eyes. Stupid, girly tears. 'I miss Mum so much. I can't understand how Dad would want anyone else around. I didn't want her to move in with us. I don't want her to act like she's Mum, but I'd been measuring her up against Mum in everything, and I'm always happy when she falls short or acts differently. That meant it's okay for me hate her.'

And when she and Dad fight and I can see how miserable it makes them, I feel guilty. Like I've wished it on them.

Cari leans forwards and brushes a hand over my arm. It's only the lightest of touches. I feel a faint buzz of warmth and caring. 'I've told you before that it makes you purple. You are very good at pulling the hurt onto yourself.'

I smile at her. She is smiling back. Then a sound from above makes us jump.

It's snow falling from a branch. Daniel is clinging to the old ladder, swinging like a piece of rag tied to a washing line.

'Daniel! I told you not to go up there!'

'Too late!' he calls back, swinging himself up. 'I can see pretty much everything!'

'There's only one thing we want to see,' I call back, but I already know the answer – he can't see Keira.

He slips.

I watch it happen in slow motion, his small body coming loose from the tree as if pulled by some unseen force and hurled, as hard as possible, at the ground. He lands with a thump. My arms are outstretched uselessly – I mean, what was I going to do, catch him? – as I run forwards. 'Are you okay? Are you?'

He grins widely at my panicked look. 'I did worse when I came off my bike doing that jump, remember? Dad grounded me for a week, but I went and tried again as soon as I got off!'

'And you landed it.' I laugh. 'Yeah, that was good work.'

'I think I hurt my knee, though,' he says, and his grimace tells me that he's hiding his pain. 'It hurts a fair bit.'

I give him a tug to his feet.

'Ah!' he yells, and I grab him just before he tumbles straight over. 'Yeah, I hurt my knee.'

'Sit down.' I brush the snow off a fallen trunk and lower him onto it. 'I told you not to.'

'Since when do I listen to you?'

He has a point. 'Okay. We'll take you home.'

'No. No way. If you do that Nina won't let you leave again.'

He has a point there, too. I look at him help-lessly. How can I leave him, hurt, alone, here in the cold? But on the other hand, how can I leave Keira out there? And Cari, I'll need her help if we find Keira. She moves so much better in the snow than I do.

'I'll be fine,' he says angrily, but his face is white. 'I'm not going to die of a busted knee.'

'You probably don't feel all the damage because of the cold,' I remind him.

'Then that's all the more reason to stay here, right? You're wasting time.'

I look at Cari. She nods slowly, and I realise that it's the only choice we've got.

Chapter 15
The Bridge

WE emerge, silent, onto Garter Street. The streetlamps are on. They line the street like a row of faint stars.

The bridge is deserted. I've never seen it like this, with the river below shrouded in mist. It seems to hang, unsuspended, in the air. It seems to lead to nowhere.

I look at Cari. She is looking straight ahead, her eyes wide.

I struggle to swallow the huge knot in my throat, and nearly choke.

Somehow, I have the telescope in my hands. I couldn't remember putting it in my pocket, and yet here it is. I raise it slowly to my eye. I almost don't want to look, because if I see what I know is there, it makes it real. I don't want it to be real.

But it is.

And the bridge is still a bridge, but it has changed. It melds, about halfway down its length, into a lattice of silver wire. The threads are stretched and torn. The road sways in a wind I can't feel. The entire structure is shivering under the strain of holding itself together. What will happen once it breaks?

I lower the telescope, and find that I no longer even need it to see the structure. It is plain before our eyes. But it's not the Garter Street Bridge. It's the bridge between our world and Shar.

'How can that bridge be here?' I say. 'How can it be seen?'

'This bridge between our worlds is failing,' says Cari. 'Even as we stand here.'

'Then what happens when it snaps? Will the cold go away? Will things go back to the way they were?'

'No.' She speaks slowly. 'No. It won't. The bridge isn't the cause of the ice, Jake. The bridge has always been here. So have hundreds of others, and more will form, or fade, as time goes on.'

'Then how can we fix this? How can we seal the boundary?'

'I have to go back, Jake.' she whispers. 'It was my fault. I wanted it so much! To see your world, to know what was out here. But I didn't want this. I didn't mean . . . I would never want to destroy . . .'

She looks at me then, beseechingly. She wills me to understand. She holds out her hand. I don't hesitate to take it.

And as my fingers clasp hers, I see it all. The falling water. The city. The beautiful ice. Men and women, as slender and pale-skinned and beautiful as her. It's paradise, it's heaven. In slow motion I see a woman smile. A small girl playing with coloured blocks. An elderly man lying on a white bed, contentment on his face as he sighs out his last breath.

'But it's so beautiful,' I say.

She nods, and leads me by the hand through these images until I see her, another version of her standing on a balcony, speaking to someone . . . a woman. It is Lena. Cari's mother.

'I want to know,' the apparition-Cari says.

'There are some things we never will understand, Cari.'

'But there is another world out there. We may not understand it, but how can we ignore it? Don't you want to know? Doesn't it burn inside you?'

'It is not ours to know, sweet one. That world was separated from us long ago.'

'But there are bridges still.'

'The bridges exist because they are needed.'

'Our link to this other place is needed, then.'

'Truthfully, child, you must not think in this way. I have told you why it must be. Their world is ruined, decimated by war, poverty, disease. They have forgotten that we even exist, so convinced are they of their uniqueness, their superiority. If they knew, they would overrun and kill us all.'

'But if the links exist, there is a reason for them! Why can I not use them? Why can I not at least see?'

And then the scene shifts. Something is happening. I am surrounded by white light, and a gasp of pain is torn from my throat. I feel the ground shift under my feet.

There, before me, is the single golden strand that I saw through the telescope. The thread leading up to Shar. It stretches out into the distance, as thin and fine as a strand of spider's silk. I reach for it. My clumsy touch doesn't break it – instead, it makes the wire hum with tension. It resonates back and forth, back and forth with a sound like a bee buzzing.

And I feel a sense of incredible achievement, an overwhelming delight that I have succeeded. I know that I'm experiencing Cari's memory.

I'm wrenched again, backwards, off my feet. Someone is shouting, screaming. There is anger, white hot and blinding, so powerful in this place where rage has no place. There is fear, too, and I know it is Cari's. She is crying.

'I had to know.'

A backwards step onto the swaying bridge.

'You can never know! You are stupid, foolish, oh you do not know how much, you cannot be allowed, this will not be allowed. Never. This must not be known.'

'No. Please. I didn't mean it. I will never . . .'

'Foolish! What you have done, the consequences – girl you can never know what you have set in motion or how it will become-'

'Please. Please. Please don't.'

The bridge sways and shudders. 'I'm sorry,' she says, and raises her hands.

'You did cause the ice.'

'I did not mean it,' she says. 'It was not my intention. I did what Mrs Henders did. I studied the bridges, every aspect of them, until I was certain I could make it work. I unravelled a strand from one of the bridges, and I pushed it through the boundary. Along it I could feel the vibrations and resonations of people's actions and emotions. Just like Mrs Henders, I thought I'd made a discovery. But the thread that I pushed through, that tiny thing . . . it made a pinprick through the veil.'

'It let a part of your world directly into ours.'

'The veils have grown so thin. There are gaps where the bridges lie, like breaks in the cloud that let sunshine through. But my thread punched a hole from one world to the other. It started to let Shar leak through. That's when the frosts would have started in your world – a few weeks ago. And when they found out what I had done . . . I was frightened. I tried to run. I stepped onto the bridge, but . . . '

'That woman cut the bridge from under you.'

'She cut the bridge. If others found out what I discovered, it would have been worse. She may have saved my life. I hate her.'

'Who is she?'

'My mother.'

I remember the rage, the horror in the woman's voice – Lena's voice, Cari's mother's voice.

Fear. And knowledge that she must give up her child for the good of her world.

'Do you despise me now?' she says. There is anger in her voice. 'As much as I despise myself? I loved this world, and for that, I have bought this disaster on you all. Those animals that are dying. Those people who are missing. Your father. Keira. This is all my fault.'

I realise then that Mrs Henders was right. Cari did cause the ice. Weeks ago, when she drew that tiny thread between our worlds, the thread Mrs Henders had seen through her telescope, she began to let Shar through. 'This is nobody's fault. You didn't mean for it to happen. But Cari, how can we undo it?'

'I must go back. I must tell them to cut the thread.'

'If you cut the thread . . .'

'The bridges will still exist, Jake. Unpredictable as they are, they will still exist.'

'Don't go,' I say suddenly. 'Cut the thread from this end.'

She dances out of reach. 'I love your world, Jake – I love the ideas, the technology, the microwaves and animations, but I know now I don't belong here. I can't do what Mrs Henders did, and get a job, and a house, and spend the rest of my life pretending. I cannot stay here.'

'What's to stop them from doing the same thing again? Like Mrs Henders said, they can just throw you back.'

She's already walking away.

'Cari!' I yell. For a heartbeat I think I have to follow her. I can walk across that shimmering bridge and into her world, into Shar. I take a step and then I stop. Daniel. Daniel is hurt and waiting for me.

I feel like I'm being torn apart.

'Cari, wait,' I call.

She doesn't even turn around. Already she's just a shape in the mist. And then she's gone. Angel girl, climbing that shimmering bridge back to the stars, where the city blazes so bright with its own light.

Chapter 16
Home

'WHERE'S Cari?' Daniel demands. When I don't answer, he reads the look in my face, and looks up at the invisible city above us. 'She's gone back.'

I nod.

'Keira . . .'

'I don't know. She could be anywhere,' I say. 'Right now I need to get you home.'

His white face is pinched. I take him under the arm and hoist him up. 'Geez you're heavy.'

We make our way slowly home.

***

Nina is apoplectic.

Of course she is. She woke up alone in a house that should have contained three kids under her care, with her partner missing and the world ending slowly outside the door. When we do arrive, it's minus one of our number, and with Daniel limping and white-faced. Her ire is completely justified. And after our talk in the plantation and my recent realisations, I find I'm glad to have someone who cares. Dad – our blood relative – didn't even know we were missing! But here is Nina, worried enough about it that she has tears in her eyes even as she's screaming blue murder in our faces.

But I still wish she wouldn't.

'Keira?' I ask her immediately.

'Keira's mum called me back to tell me Keira had been found in the hospital.'

I feel weak at the knees with relief.

She turns to face me. 'Did Rebecca get home safely?'

It's the strangest way of asking the question. I nod slowly. 'Yes.'

I hope I'm not lying about that.

Daniel is stripped and examined. 'It's a sprain,' she pronounces, and dumps a packet of Children's Panadol in front of him. 'We'll take you in for some x-rays, but it can wait until the snow clears up. We'd be risking worse than that on the roads now.'

I'm expecting her to start shouting again, but she shakes her head. And she sits down at the table, suddenly very quiet. Daniel and I look at each other.

'God, you kids,' she says. 'There's a huge backlog of patients at the hospital, apparently, which is why it took them so long to get in touch with Keira's parents. Keira's mum told me she'd spoken to you, Jake. It wasn't until then I realised where you'd gone. I knew you'd gone to try and find her. I knew you'd have to try.'

'If we told you, you'd try and stop us.' I don't want to say it, but it slips out. 'This was one problem that doesn't have age limits attached.'

Nina's face is pinched and tired. She looks old. I wonder when I started to know her well enough to even notice that.

'But Keira's okay.'

'It's not serious,' she says. 'A broken leg, that's all. A rescue team found her early this morning. She'd been out there all night, but her warm clothing protected her.'

I actually do sink to the floor, then, and just sit there for a while.

***

Nina makes Milo and we sit in front of the TV under a doona, not watching a thing. It's nearly lunch time when the door slams open. Dad strides in.

'Dad!' yells Daniel, dragging the doona with him as he jumps up, but stops short of hugging him, in exactly the way a ten-year-old realises they shouldn't be acting childishly. Dad looks rumpled and shadowed, obviously having slept in his clothes.

Nina, though, takes one look at his worn face and wraps her arms tightly around him.

Me, I'm pretty tempted to do the same.

***

It's a weird sort of day. We all seem to cling together, none of us really wanting to be alone. The house feels small, as if it's been warped somehow. I try to read. I try to do homework. I try to play computer games. I can't concentrate on any of them.

Daniel sits on my bed, looking through the window.

'There could be lots of people out there like Mrs Henders, couldn't there?' he says wonderingly. 'People from Shar who are pretending to be normal.'

'Yeah, maybe,' I say.

'Do you reckon we could go there? If we found a bridge?'

'Yeah,' I reply. 'I guess we could. But we'd be locked away if we did.'

The phone rings a couple of times. Mostly it's friends and family checking up to make sure everyone's doing okay, but every time, I creep from wherever I am to listen. I dread that stupid phone. I almost want to take it off the hook, so that no one can call with good news or bad.

I wander down to the kitchen with the vague idea that I'm hungry and having something to eat might help. They're in there, Dad and Nina, and I stop outside the door. Their voices are angry, restrained – the type of voice that makes you wish they'd just shout it all out loud instead of tiptoeing around.

'... not what you really want,' Nina is saying. 'That's all.'

'No,' he says. 'I shouldn't have to justify that –'

'You don't. You don't have to do anything. But don't forget that this doesn't just concern you – it's my problem too. Not to mention Daniel and Jake. You have to stop ignoring us.'

'I'm not!' He takes a deep breath. 'Look, I'm really tired, and I know how stressed you are. This whole situation is not going to be improved by our current moods.'

Nina slams something – a mug? The kettle? – onto the table. Not hard, but enough to make a noise. 'Don't you dare walk away from this! You can't keep doing that.'

There is a long silence. 'I broke my nail,' says Nina in a small, choked sort of voice. I lean around the jamb so that I can see her, sitting at the table, staring at her finger, laughing and sobbing at the same time. And Dad – he's grinning widely, and wrapping his arms around her from behind.

'I've got a meeting next week,' he says. 'But they think it's a pretty sure thing that I'll get the promotion. It means I can do more of my work from home and I can delegate some cases to other people. I won't have to take as many phone calls or sort out as many emails. I'm sorry I haven't been around. But this is what I wanted, and what I needed. Things will get better from now on. I promise.'

***

'Where's Rebecca?' It's Keira's first question as I walk into her hospital room. There are flowers on the shelf and a box of chocolates open beside the bed. And Keira, lying down, looks nothing like Keira at all. If she's not bouncing off the walls she's unrecognisable.

'Hey.' I'm a bit uneasy. I don't really know how to speak to her. In the time between now and when I saw her last so much has happened. I can barely remember sitting with her in our kitchen just yesterday. She's a stranger.

'Oh, don't you dare ask me if I'm feeling okay, or if it hurt, or any of that crap. I've told the story a hundred times. I slipped in a gutter, okay? It was stupid and unexciting. An SEC volunteer found me and got me back to a check-in point. They took me to the hospital. So, where's Rebecca?'

'She's gone home,' I tell her. 'She was only visiting.'

She looks disappointed. 'She should have said goodbye. I like her. Is she coming back?'

'I don't think so, not any time soon.' I can tell her the truth about this, at least.

'Well, that sucks. You made a good couple.'

I feel all the blood in my body rush into my cheeks. 'We weren't . . .'

'Whatever, Miles. Oh, geez, if I don't get out of this bed soon I'm going to go nuts.'

I grin. 'I've got an idea.'

I beg a nurse for a wheelchair. We take off through the hallways. 'Faster!' Keira urges. Her need for recklessness has not been tamed by her adventure. We careen down the ramps, narrowly miss a lunch cart, and find ourselves outside.

The snow has mostly melted by now. There are still fuzzy white patches in the corners of the garden beds, and most of the treeferns and flowers are dead. It's like this all over the city. A lot of people have been injured and hurt, not to mention the wildlife. The insurance companies are having to pay out big time for cars and houses. Our school won't open until next week because of damage to the roof.

But slowly things are returning to normal.

'There goes our project,' says Keira. 'A-plus material down the drain. Couldn't the cold snap have held on for just a few more days? We could have gotten more examples. Our own personal case study.'

'People were dying, Keira,' I remind her. But she's not thinking about that.

'Maybe we could do something else instead. Like . . . how guys are so unbelievable. I can't believe Baz.'

'What happened?'

'We kind of broke up.'

'What?' I'm surprised.

'Well, he broke up with me. He sounded like he was quoting every soppy break-up line he's ever heard in movies. Boys are so . . .' She looks at me and laughs. 'Nah, not you, Miles. I don't mean you. I reckon if you ever broke up with someone it would be for a real reason.'

She looks at me and I try to hide my thoughts.

'You miss her, don't you?'

'Yeah,' I say. I can't say anything else.

'It'd make a good project, you know. We could include snippets on adult relationships, as well. Like your dad.'

I shake my head. 'I think Dad and Nina are going to be okay, you know.'

'What changed?'

'I don't know,' I say. 'But Dad found one of Nina's brochures. There's plenty of appeals for clothing and stuff after the damage that was caused by the ice. Some people lost their entire house. So Dad said there was plenty of good stuff in boxes in the garage, if Nina wouldn't mind sorting it out.'

Keira huffs her surprise. 'Your mum's stuff?'

'Yeah,' I say. 'But I don't think I'd mind.'

Keira nods. 'Your Mum was always helping out with school fundraisers and stuff. She's the first person who would have given stuff out if it was needed. You know, once she told me this story about guardian angels. She said we each had one watching over us.' She pauses, looks at me. 'It sounds stupid, but I reckon that's why I didn't die out there. My guardian angel was looking after me. Or something.'

'Yeah,' I grin. 'Do you want to go back inside?'

'No. Don't you dare take me inside. I swear, when I get my leg back I'll kick your arse.'

So we go and see how well a wheelchair can handle doughnuts on the icy concrete outside the front entrance instead.

Mrs Henders' telescope feels heavy and warm in my pocket.

I'm thinking that when I get home I'll have to call Baz. Maybe we can work on some kicking techniques before next soccer practice.

Thank you for reading
The City of Silver Light,
we hope you enjoyed it.

If you would like to be kept informed of
further releases in *The Bridges Trilogy,* or
other new books from Hague Publishing, why
not subscribe to our newsletter at:

www.HaguePublishing.com/subscribe

And if you loved the book and have a moment
to spare we would really appreciate a short
review. Your help in spreading the word
would be gratefully received.

EXTRACT FROM

ACROSS THE BRIDGE OF ICE

BOOK 2 IN THE BRIDGES TRILOGY

BY

Ruth Fox

ACROSS THE BRIDGE OF ICE

Rarely do you find a book written from the teenage perspective that resonates so well.

Karen Fainges

I loved the beautiful prose, the wonderful descriptions of everything . . . and really loved the story line.

Christina – Ensconced in Lit

An amazing fantasy novel . . . this one will appeal to a large audience; young and not-so-young alike. Highly recommended.

Brenda – Goodreads Top Reviewer

Chapter 1
The Worst Thing in the World

THERE'S a doctor in Outpatients who looks like Count Dracula. Pale skin and black hair pulled back into a bun so tight she can't even blink. I swear all she needs is a black cloak and a pair of bloodstained fangs.

'You need to take things more slowly, Keira,' she says to me every time I go in to see her. I think it's a threat.

See, I'm not a good patient. I'm *imp*atient. I find it hard to sit still, which is not good when you've got a broken ankle. Most of the time I'm doing stuff I'm not supposed to, like, you know, *walking*. And . . . well, falling down the front steps.

'I am taking things slowly,' I tell her.

I resist the urge to pick at the neatly folded sheet covering the bed underneath me. Being in this room, with all the neatly arranged equipment and dark furniture, always makes me feel antsy. It probably doesn't help that I haven't slept properly in ages. I keep having dreams about ice. It crackles all over the house, and into the trees, and across the grass and the streets before everything turns white. But as much as I hate seeing doctors, I *definitely* don't want to be sent to a psychologist, so I'll keep those dreams to myself.

'I didn't fall on purpose.'

Mum speaks up. 'I keep telling her she needs to take it easy. But every time I turn my back, she's out of bed making cereal or playing with the dog. And now this . . .'

I feel sorry for my mum. She works long hours running the Cassidy Heights Bakery, and has to be up at four o'clock most mornings. Not to mention the accounts, bills, sales targets, and production quotas she has to meet. Having me home from school has only given her more to worry about.

When a blizzard hit our little suburb of Cassidy Heights two weeks ago, I kind of got lost walking back from my friend Jake's place. I tripped on a kerb and went for a slide on my butt. Yeah, it wasn't exactly my shining moment. Volunteer rescue workers from the State Emergency Service found me eventually, but by the time they called my mum, she was already beyond panic.

The weather system that caused the freak snowstorm has broken up now – according to Chanel Seven News and Weather, that is. Of course, there still haven't been any satisfactory explanations about what exactly caused it. I can just picture the meteorologists at the

Weather Bureau scratching their heads. And me, I was kind of planning to get an A+ on my science project about predicting the effects of an arctic winter in a desert country, but I've kind of left my partner, Jake, in the lurch while I'm spending all this time recovering.

'Well, we'll see what these new x-rays show us.' Doctor Dracula waves a sealed yellow envelope. 'Then we'll know whether you'll be able to head back to school. Bet you'll be excited to see your friends again.' She rips open the envelope, tipping a couple of plastic sheets into her hands.

I give her a withering stare. Why do adults assume that school is some fun place where you get to hang out with your friends? It's totally not like that. Teachers spend all their time getting you not to talk, not to sit next to your friends, and not to waste time socialising. I hate school. I hate the rules and regulations.

'All I really want to do is get back to soccer practice.'

'Hm,' says Doctor Dracula. She sticks the x-ray pictures on a lighted board. It's an ominous 'hm', a sound that means *there's something bad here.*

I look at my bones. The inside of people's bodies is pretty interesting. I mean, all those little bits and pieces that join together to make us work. It's kind of fascinating what living beings are made up of.

'What's "hm"?' I ask.

Mum leans forwards, her brow crinkling.

'What we have here is a non-union,' says Doctor Dracula. 'The gap between the broken edges of the bone was a large one, and that fall you took probably pulled it further out of alignment. The bone isn't healing the way it should.'

'What does that mean?' Mum sounds worried.

'Well, we might be looking at an operation. We'd need to insert a bolt to keep the bone in place while it heals.'

'That sounds drastic.' Mum's voice is shaking a little.

'It's a relatively simple procedure, and certainly not uncommon. But I won't lie to you. There can be complications.'

'Complications – like what?' I ask.

'Well, Keira, you may have some pain in that foot for the rest of your life. Also a certain weakness. The bones will never heal as strongly as they were before they were broken.'

'But that won't matter, right? I mean, it's not like I won't be able to walk or anything.' My own voice is shaking a bit now.

'Of course you'll be able to walk. But you may find it difficult or painful to run. You might be restricted in more strenuous activities.'

Slowly, very slowly, it's dawning on me. 'What about soccer?'

She purses her lips. 'We won't rule anything out at this stage, of course. But I'd like to schedule the operation as soon as possible. Mrs

Leichman, we'll need you to fill out some forms
. . .'

I don't hear anything else. My mind is ringing with thoughts. What if, what if . . . *what if I
can never play soccer again?*

'I'll see you on Thursday, Keira,' says Doctor
Dracula.

I nod, resigned, and grab my crutches to follow Mum out of the office.

We get all the way back through the waiting
room, through the delay at reception while they
sort out some mismatching Medicare numbers,
through the slow walk down the disabled ramp
at the front door, and the short walk to the car
before she starts on me.

'Why don't you ever listen to me? You
shouldn't have been moving around. You
shouldn't have tried to manage those stairs on
your own. If you would just do what you were
told for once . . . '

'Don't yell at me!' I shout.

'I don't know how else to get you to listen!
You're too stubborn for your own good!'

'I'm the one who might never be able to run
again. I think *I'm* the one who should be upset.'

'Oh, really? Wait until you're old enough to
be responsible for someone. Then you might
understand.'

We drive home in stony silence. I hobble on
my crutches through the yard and into my
room where I slump on my bed. My door has a
busted hinge and doesn't shut properly. I count

to three, then sure enough Molly, our dog, noses her way into the room and heaves herself up on my bed. She nuzzles up beside me, her warm body solid and comforting against my side.

'Good girl, Molly,' I whisper automatically, scratching her ears just where she likes it. Her paw twitches in response.

'Keira?' Mum taps at my door. It swings slightly back and forth but she doesn't come in. 'Keira, honey, can I come in?'

'No.'

'I'm going to get some Chinese takeaway for tea. I thought you could invite a friend, if you want.'

It's a peace offering. She knows it's my favourite. But I'm not hungry. 'Alright.'

'It'll be okay, honey,' she calls softly. I hear her footsteps recede to the kitchen, where I know she'll be making a cup of coffee and staring blankly at the wall. It's just been the two of us since Dad left three years ago. We know each other's thoughts like mind-readers.

With a sigh, I roll over and reach for my bag. I pull out my phone and bring up my contacts list. I select the first number on recent calls. It rings once, twice, three times.

'Hello?' says a familiar voice.

'Jake?' I say, then burst into tears.

Chapter 2
The Almost Kiss

JAKE has been my friend since we were in primary school. We ate dog biscuits out of the packet in my garage, sat at the back of the class and punched each other in the shoulder until the teacher wrote our names on the board, and painted each other's hair green in Art. My mum and I were at the hospital on the day his little brother was born. I remember Mum holding Mrs Miles's hand as she was wheeled through the doors into the private room.

Later, when Daniel was older, all three of us spent hours playing hide-and-seek in the pine plantation in Phoenix Park. We built a tree-house in one of the tallest trees of the plantation. You could see the entire world from up there, though the treehouse must be falling to bits by now.

I guess we've drifted apart a bit lately, though. That's what happens when you grow up. I mean, I started going out with Andrew, who didn't really like Jake much. And then there was Baz, and Jake got all awkward about him and me. I wonder if he was jealous. That just makes me feel weird though – I mean Jake is my friend.

Then he met Rebecca, a really pretty, strange, pale girl who stayed with him a couple of days. And he changed. There was something strange about her but Jake never really wanted to talk about her much. I guess he was sorry she only stayed for a few days. Maybe he was really in love with her. And *that* made me feel weird, because I didn't want Jake Miles to be in love with anyone. And what does *that* mean? Is it just because he's my friend and I don't want him to drift further away?

Tonight, he turns up on the porch at eight, and Mum lets him into the lounge room where I'm propped on the couch with pillows and the TV remote, my foot on the coffee table. We eat our Chinese food and Mum goes to bed, leaving us to watch a re-run of *How I Met Your Mother*. Canned laughter echoes from the TV.

'So,' says Jake.

'So,' I reply, picking bits of fried rice off my jumper. 'It's Mikhal's birthday on the weekend. He's having a party on Saturday.'

'You reckon you can –?'

I shoot him one of my best death-glares. 'Of course I can make it. I'm not going to stop *living*.'

'Right, sorry. I was just wondering if your mum would actually let you go. She seems pretty . . . anxious.'

'I told her Mikhal's parents would be there. I also told her I'll just sit on the couch the whole night, because it hurts too much to move anyway. I think she feels bad about the operation, bad enough that she'll let me have a treat beforehand. Besides, I haven't seen Mikhal or any of the others in ages. It's bad for me, psychologically, to be so isolated.'

I bat my eyelids innocently and Jake laughs.

'Cool. Well, I'll ask Dad. I think Nina can drive us. She's been talking to Mikhal's mum a lot, about all this charity stuff – and your mum will be sleeping, won't she?'

I nod. Mum has early nights. 'That'll make things easier. She likes Nina.'

I'm not sure about Nina myself. Every time I see her walking around Jake's house, cooking in the kitchen, cleaning the bathroom, reading in the lounge room, I just picture Mrs Miles, Jake's real mum. Even though it's been years since Mrs Miles died, it just seems wrong to have someone else in her place. For a long time, Jake hated her with a passion, but since the night of the blizzard, he's been warming up to her. I reckon we all got closer that night, so I'm obligated to make an effort to do the same.

'I've gotta go,' Jake says at last. 'I told Dad I'd be home by nine-thirty.'

'Jeez, talk about a curfew.'

'I've got school tomorrow. Or have you forgotten some of us still have to go to class, you lazy bum?'

'I'm not a lazy bum!' I yell, punching him in the arm. He leans over to whack me in the shoulder, but all of a sudden he's too close – his face inches from mine. I can see his lips. I can *taste* his lips. It would take only the slightest movement to kiss him. I could kiss him. For a second it's going to happen. He's going to lean in and kiss me.

My heart is racing. My breath catches in my throat and I pull back – and tumble right off the couch with a yelp.

'Shit!' Jake gasps, catching me in his arms. My breath leaves me. He's strong – strong enough to lift me easily. 'Shit, I'm sorry! Are you okay?'

'Ouch,' I grit my teeth against the pain. My ankle feels like it's on fire.

He lifts me back up to the couch. Something has fallen out of his pocket and digs into my leg.

'What's this?' I pick it up. It's a slender tube made of brass or something heavy. There's thick glass in both ends. It's an old-fashioned telescope. As I touch it, something jumps in me. Like a spark of static electricity, it runs right through me, leaving my hair tingling.

Jake grabs it – I mean, full on snatches it – right out of my hands. 'It's nothing.'

The moment of the almost-kiss is gone. There's no getting it back now. This, whatever this is, has wiped it from existence. 'Why are you carrying around an old telescope?'

'What does that matter?' He tucks the thing back in his pocket, avoiding my eyes. 'Are you okay? Should I get your mum?'

'No. She'll be asleep by now. I'm fine.'

'I'll call you before Saturday,' Jake says quickly, pretty much running out the door.

More laughter blares from the TV. I don't notice anything that happens for the rest of the episode because I'm thinking about Jake. Somehow, he's not just "Miles" anymore. When did I start thinking of him as Jake?

About The Author

RUTH Fox is the author of *The Bridges Trilogy* and the award-winning *Monster-boy: Lair of the Grelgoroth*.

She loves to paint, cook and play computer games (very badly). She has a Bachelor of Arts/Diploma of Arts in Professional Writing and Editing. So far she has worked at several far less meaningful or interesting jobs — but writing is her life. She loves science fiction, fantasy, romance, adventure, young adult, adult, literature, old books, new books, and everything in between.

She currently lives with her husband and three very curious and adventurous sons (who also love books) in Ballarat, Victoria.

You can visit her website at ruth-fox.com or on Facebook at RuthFoxAuthorandArtist.

Hague

Publishing

www.HaguePublishing.com
PO Box 451 Bassendean
Western Australia 6934